I0626517

Printed in the United States of America

First Printing, 2019

ISBN: 978-0-9971187-1-1

abconeauthor.com

PanHead

Enjoy the goings-on with the group at PanHead Custom Harley Shop & Motorcycle Repair. You can't help but fall in love with this group of men and women. Their smart mouth and quirky sense of humor will always get you.

In this first book of the PanHead Group series, Hunter Clark, had resigned to the fact he would only have two women in his life, his sister and aunt and he was fine with that. He sure in the hell wasn't expecting another woman to change what he thought his fated life would be.

Stephanie Pierce, was at a crossroad in her life. Recently quitting her graphic design job that she loved only because her supervisor hands thought her butt was his to play with—until she punched him in the face. Her life had consisted of her career, family, and her Harley-Davidson. And that was it. She was happy and didn't think she needed anything else. But when she practically ran into Hunter Clark at his shop - Fate took over.

PanHead

The panhead was a Harley-Davidson motorcycle engine, so nicknamed because of the distinct shape of the rocker covers. The engine replaced the knucklehead engine in 1948 and was manufactured until 1965 when it was replaced by the shovelhead.

Harley-Davidson engines evolved through the years, with its particular shape of the valve covers has allowed Harley enthusiasts to classify an engine simply by looking at the shape of the covers resembling an upside-down pan.

PanHead

PanHead Group Series-Book One
A. B. CONE

DEDICATION

To those that kept asking me about my novel and getting me to *man-up* and get it out there. Also, to my family, you all are the love and light of my life.

CHAPTER ONE

It was in situations like this that Hunter Clark wished there were two of him. At the very moment he was stuck on Highway One, twenty miles from home, at a dead stop, trying to calm down a horse. Yes, you read right, calming a scared, malnourished, horse on the highway.

You would think a car accident had caused this snarled traffic jam. But oh no, traffic had stopped because of a horse who ran onto the highway. Miraculously the cars in front had seen the horse ahead of time and had slowed down to a stop, Hunter's truck being one of those vehicles.

About an hour later the local radio station reported that the runaway horse had gotten away from its owner, who apparently had just finished looping a rope around the horse's neck when it decided to escape. Good thing too, the newscaster had said because the owner was getting the horse ready to take it to the vet's to have it put down. The owner's ranch was right off the freeway with a broken-down fence that surrounded his property.

Hunter closed his cell phone after making a call to his aunt. He had asked her if she would go in his place to his sister's parent-teacher conference. Thank God for his Aunt Milly, she was a godsend for him. She always came through.

Standing on the side of the highway with the horse, Hunter finally watched his truck being moved by CHP farther down from the scene. From the beginning of the mishap to the end had taken four and a half hours. Traffic had gradually moved, but in less than five minutes it slowed again as gawkers drove by to get a look at the horse. A horse trailer blocked the view as it...finally...arrived and pulled to the side of the highway.

Hunter heard about the horse's fate, made an impulsive decision and offered to rescue the filly for his sister. He already had a horse, so another one wouldn't be a problem.

Hunter watched a sheriff's car arrive. Hunter figured that the person who stepped out of the backseat of the patrol car was the owner of the horse. Hunter was standing close enough to hear everything that was said.

The scruffy-looking old man with raggedy gray hair reluctantly agreed to his offer only because handcuffs were being put on him and he faced a hefty fine for animal cruelty. But, unfortunately it wasn't that easy. The SPCA (Society for the Prevention of Cruelty to Animals, Santa Cruz, CA) was involved now and soon the courts would be too. Didn't matter, Hunter was willing to take over as the new owner when everything was approved.

The horse trailer finally pulled out into the slow-moving traffic, taking the filly to her temporary home. Before Hunter started his truck up he called his Aunt Milly to explained the full story and letting her know he was on his way home.

***

Hunter's mind flashed back to his parents. They had him when they were so young, four months after they gotten married. He grew up with them always showing some type of affection toward each other. His parents, were shocked when his mom found out she was pregnant, since the odds of her getting pregnant at that age was small. Or so she thought. But the loss of his mother to cancer some years back, at the young age, with his father, dying just months later of a broken heart was a shock for Hunter. He was twenty years old and now had the responsibility of raising his one year old sister, Anne.

When Hunter's parents died, he was engaged. It wasn't soon after when his engagement broke off. The so-called engagement was doomed anyway. What the hell was he thinking? His ex-fiancee had no interest in helping to raise Anne, much less any child from Hunter. This was a surprise; she had told him earlier when dating she wanted a family.

His Aunt Milly, stepped in. She was Hunter's father's youngest sister of eight siblings. She moved in with them to help Hunter raise Anne. There was only eight years difference between him and his aunt. Aunt Milly was a lifesaver. She had always been there for him. He owed her so much.

Hunter was now thirty years old, Anne eleven. Together, he and his Aunt Milly, were doing a damn good job. And he was proud of his little sister.

Hunter sold his parents house a couple of years after their death.With Aunt Milly's help he bought a large lot that had two houses on it along Highway Nine. It wasn't too long after that when Hunter and his best friend, Jake Daniels, started their motorcycle business: PanHead Harley Custom Shop & Motorcycle Repair. It was located in the front part of the lot, along Highway 9, with the houses set in the back. Hunter and Anne lived in the first house; Aunt Milly living in the smaller one.

Anne and Aunt Milly were the only positive experience Hunter had had when it came to the opposite sex. His last relationship, with a woman named Jenny, had turned into a nightmare. After that drama, there was no room for any other woman. Hunter was happy with what he had. Sure, he had over night flings here and there, but nothing more.

Hunter finally arrived home. Steering the truck towards the front of his house, he saw Anne, run out of the house, shouting out questions regarding the "poor horse." Once Hunter settled Anne down he told her that as soon as they had the courts approval, the horse would be living with them. Anne was ecstatic. She was finally getting a horse she'd been wanting.

Jumping up and down with excitement, Anne asked.

"Hunter, when can I see her? Can I name her? When will she be coming home?"

"Sweetheart, it will probably take a few months before you can see the horse. Right now she's probably being seen by a vet and then she'll be taken care of by the Santa Cruz SPCA. Why don't you go make a list of names for your filly. You might want to wait before you make your final decision though. She's in bad shape right now. Once she starts gaining weight, she'll definitely look different. What do say, kiddo?"

"I can't wait, I'm going to start my list now."

Anne ran back into the house and Aunt Milly walked out. She updated Hunter on what had been said at the parent-teacher conference, which he knew would be positive. His sister was one of the school's star pupils.

"Well, I'm off like a herd of turtles. Oh, I forgot to tell ya, Hunter, dinner is in the oven for you guys. Tonight is poker night with the girls."

Aunt Milly turned around and head back to her little place.

"Thanks, Aunt Mil, as always you're a life saver."

"That's what I'm here for. Love you too."

Lifting her arm in a wave, she headed toward her cottage, which was only a few hundred feet from Hunter's house.

Hunter's Aunt Milly was a character. Butt-ass honest, sassy as hell, with a great sense of humor. She was still waiting for Mr. Right, but in no hurry. At first he didn't understand why she wasn't hitched already, but as the years went by he realized she was either holding off either until he found someone or until Anne graduated from high school. He was close to his aunt when he was growing up, but it seemed like they had bonded even more when his parents, (Milly's brother and sister-in-law) had died one right after the other. Being a successful author, Milly was able to write at home and still watch over Anne when Hunter needed her. Hunter felt bad that his aunt had put a halt to her social life for her nephew and niece. He knew if he ever brought the subject up she wouldn't talk about it. She would have it no other way. That was his Milly.

No sooner had Hunter and Anne finished cleaning the dinner dishes than his cell phone rang. It was Jake Daniels, his best friend and co-owner of PanHead Custom Harley Shop & Motorcycle Repair.

Hunter put the cell phone to his ear.

"Yo."

"Hey, man, can I grab you for a couple of hours.Your expertise is needed over here? A bike needs the gas tank put on and the owner is coming by to check the paint job tomorrow. Spike ended up puking in the bathroom, so I sent him home. The flu season has gotten his sorry ass but good. Oh and also, tomorrow I have to leave to deliver Butch's bike. Since Spike is too sick to do it and Rob and Paula are still on vacation, that leaves you to be here while I'm gone. So would you mind also bringing your ass over here from eleven a.m. to two p.m. tomorrow?"

"Not a problem." Hunter replied. "Give me a few minutes to figure out who Anne wants to hang with and tomorrow I'll be there around ten a.m."

"Great. Thanks Hunt, see you in ten tomorrow."

Hunter walked into Anne's room and gave her a choice of where she could wait: the shop, or Milly's house? Anne chose the shop. It was no hardship: both had a PlayStation 3 console and cable TV.

CHAPTER TWO

Anne walked into the Harley shop. Loving how even though the guys here dealt with a lot of grease, the place was kept clean. Everything was always in its place. There were no posters of naked woman; that would have made her feel uncomfortable. But what she really loved was all the Harley paraphernalia hanging on the walls along with award-winning pictures of some of their bikes.

Jake bent down as she ran up to him and gave him a hug and a kiss.

"Hey, beautiful, how's my favorite godchild?"

"Jake, I'm your only godchild and I'm fine. Did Hunter tell you about the horse he rescued?"

Puzzled, he looked at Hunter.

"Horse? Rescued? Explain."

Before Hunter could reply Anne turned and walked toward the office, leaving them to talk. Hunter explained all that happened that day.

When he finished, Jake let out a long whistle.

"Man, today was not your day, huh? Although you will probably be getting a horse for all your troubles. That's a positive."

"Yeah, this filly was so malnourished I'm not sure how she has survived this long. But she did. Anne is already making a list of names for the her."

"Well, she has been bugging you for her own horse for a

while and it seems like she now has one."

"Yeah, it looks like it. Where's the gas tank you want me to put on?"

Jake showed Hunter the chopped 72 Sportster panhead with an extended front-end, which was ready and waiting for the gas tank to be put on.

As soon as Hunter saw the gas tank he whistled.

"This is going to be one sweet-looking bike once everything is done. I like the idea of the design. Whose idea was it?"

"Well, before Paula and Robert left on their vacation, Paula said the owner of the bike gave her the design she had created for the gas tank and Paula made it happen. You know, Hunter, we have some talented people working for us."

"Don't I know it. Have you had any luck in finding a designer?"

"No, the portfolios that I've seen so far are not what either one of us want, so the position is still open. And you know me, since I'm Mr. Positive, the right person will come along at the right time."

Hunter laughed.

"Yeah, well, I don't doubt you anymore since you have proven me wrong numerous times. So I'm content to wait."

Hunter went to work to finish one of the bikes Spike was working on along with attaching the gas tank to the good-looking 72 Sportster. It took about an hour and a half to finish what needed to be done. Good thing, since it was already 9:30 p.m. and Anne had nodded off in front of the TV.

One positive about the shop, you could walk to it from Hunter's house. PanHead was located next to Hunter's long driveway on Highway 9 amongst the majestic redwood trees. Behind the shop, Hunter's and Aunt Milly's house is on a large four acre lot, with the shop being part of the acres. Since their driveway was long heading to the house, tonight Hunter brought his truck in case Anne fell asleep and she did.

CHAPTER THREE

Hunter felt good. He had slept well and was looking forward to the new day he'd whistled a tune as he put eggs and bacon on a plate.

He yelled for Anne.

"Anne, breakfast..."

He was unable to finish what he was going to say because Anne came walking into the kitchen with a big smile on her face and replied.

"Is ready."

"OK, young lady, you've got twenty minutes to eat and head outside to catch the bus."

She laughed.

"Hunter, do you realize you tell me that every time you fix me breakfast?"

"Sorry, sweetheart, it's an old habit to break. But I also wanted to mention that most of today I'll be in the shop. Your welcome to drop by and hang out after school or head over to Aunt Milly's."

"OK, but I think I'll go see how Aunt Milly's poker night with the ladies went. They always seem to have so much fun. The last time I stayed with Auntie all I could hear was the constant laughing. I don't have any idea what they were talking about since I was in the guest room, but I was laughing anyway. You know, Aunt Milly says laughing is one of her hobbies and I can see why. It made me feel good listening to those women laughing with me laughing along with them."

"When I was your age, Aunt Milly and I went to see the Disney movies *The Rescuers* and *The Rescuers Down Under* and we both laughed our heads off. I remember how good it felt. I hope you always enjoy the light side of life, like Jake. That man refuses to let anything get him down."

"Oh, I won't, Hunter. That is one of the reasons why Jake is so much fun to be with, don't you think?"

"Yeah, I have to agree with you on that. So now that you're practically inhaled your breakfast, time to head out and wait for the bus. I put your lunch in your backpack already and it's your fave, peanut butter and jelly, with extra jelly, right?"

"Right. Thanks, Hunt, see you this afternoon. Bye."

With that Anne walked out toward the bus stop, which luckily was in front of the shop heading south on Highway. 9.

Pretty soon Anne would be starting junior high, which had started to make Hunter nervous. Even without makeup his sister was going to be a beauty with her long dark brown hair and pretty face. He knew once she gave the boys her beautiful smile they would be goners. Thank God right now Anne was too busy with reading, her friends and Hunter's horse, Blaze, to start turning her interest to boys. Hunter didn't even want to contemplate the idea of that happening.

***

Hunter was in the shop and had just hung up the phone after writing down an order of another repair job that would be brought in Saturday, when Rob and Paula would be back from vacation. Jake was the one who delegated the jobs among the crew. Hunter did the books, unless work was needed on a bike, but he left the shop's internal affairs to Jake, who was more of a people person anyway. People warmed up to him a lot faster than they did to, Hunter, which was fine with him.

Hunter was more of a behind-the-scenes kind of guy. He would rather not have the attention on him, where Jake could care less. That is why Hunter always could be found in the office. Going by the attention Jake received from women, that man was one calm, cool, collected guy, though Hunter would never tell him that for fear the man's ego would expand close to exploding. And everyone who worked with him would definitely not want that to happen.

Hunter had just finished paying bills when he heard a female voice called out.

"Hello, anyone here?"

***

Hunter yelled.

"Hold on, I'll be right out."

He walked around the desk and out of the office only to practically run into a goddess in blue jeans. Hunter and the stranger ended up about a foot away from one another and he immediately felt some kind of energy sizzling between the two of them. Hunter was shocked by his response, because he just didn't do sizzle, never has. So what the hell was this?

"Oh my God, I apologize," the woman said. "I heard a voice and it led me here. I have an appointment with Spike to check out the paint job on the gas tank. Is he here?"

She looked around to see if anyone else was in the shop.

Hunter was able to come to his senses once this beauty turned her head toward the shop.

"Spike ended up with the flu and went home, but I'm here to show you the bike. My name is Hunter and it's nice meeting you."

"Well, thank you. I'm Stephanie Pierce . Please lead the way."

***

Stephanie was hoping to break the damn charge that was still emitting between them. She didn't know what was going on?

She stepped aside so this gorgeous hunk of man could pass. He was a sight to behold. She had to remind herself there was no way she was interested or wanted to be interested. She thought of her last date she'd gone out with, if that's what you wanted to call Curt. Mistake was the correct word. No thanks, been there done that.

Yeah, well if only this fine piece in front of her would bat for the other side, it would make life so much more easier, although there was a big *doubt it* there. But, if he did bat for the other side, women of the earth would lower their heads and mourn. He was that spectacular. A million other women would have to agree that this tall, dark haired, sexy man would probably make it easy to forget your troubles, well, at least for a little while.

She would say he was six foot three of fine. All muscle and the sexiest face she has ever seen on a man. His thick dark brown hair had thin streaks of gold that had a slight wave cut. His intense green eyes took her breath away. She knew those eyes of his held a mystery that she would love to solve.

She reminded herself she didn't need or want a relationship. She had no time and no energy. But, man, what a walk. Since when did she noticed the way a man walked? He was wearing jeans and why was it that jeans always seemed to bring out the best when it came to asses. This guy had one of the nicest asses she had ever seen. Oh boy, this was not good.

Hunter led her to the 72 Sportster with its newly painted gas tank he had put on earlier.

"What do you think of the paint job."

"My God, it's better than I had expected."

"You know, the thin white lines that outline the solid black tank was a good idea. Not only that, the extra thin light blue along the white line really adds to its appeal. I am told that was your design."

"Yeah, I've been wanting to do that and since black is my favorite color, I knew this simple line would bring out its appeal even more."

"Are you a designer by trade?"

"Well, unfortunately, I was, but just recently I'm unemployed, so I'm looking into other area's of employment. Design work is so highly competitive and it seems like once you find a design position the turnover is low."

"So tell me, if you don't mind me asking, why are you not working at your prior place of employment?"

"I left the job due to personal reasons and it had nothing to due with my talent as a designer."

"Well, I was really impressed with this simple yet sharp design. You see, we have been looking for a designer and haven't had any kind of luck yet. So why don't you take an application home and give Jake a call later this afternoon, around four p.m. You guys can figure out when to meet and greet."

Stephanie was elated.

"Are you kidding me? Boy, talk about being in the right place at the right time. I would love a chance to show you two my work."

Stephanie was beside herself. *What were the odds?* Although she knew she probably was up against some tough competition, she was more than game for it.

CHAPTER FOUR

"When you talk to Jake, would you mind if you left your portfolio overnight so I can also look at your designs? I'm not always here in the office, but I would like to see the rest of your work."

"Oh, that would be no problem. Thank you. But to change the subject, when do you think my bike will be done?"

"From what I have seen and read from the worksheet, Spike finished the tune-up and there are just has a few minor tweaks he needs to do with the seat and he also needs to take it out on a test drive. So when you talk to Jake later this afternoon he'll be able to give you an idea of when and what time to pick it up."

"I'm so excited, I can't wait to take Pearl home."

"Pearl?"

Smiling at Hunter.

"My bike. I named her Pearl. I didn't think Sally or Nelly would fit."

"No, not Sally and definitely not Nelly. You picked the name for the soft, sleekness of the black pearl, huh?" Hunter lowered his head only to lift his eyes, giving her one hot look.

"Yep, that's right."

Stephanie knew she had to get out of there soon because she was starting to tingle in places she didn't want to tingle.

"Well, she's a thing of beauty. You did good."

"Well, thanks, but I'd better head out. I'll give Jake a call later this afternoon. Thanks, Hunter. See ya."

She turned around and headed out the door, feeling Hunter's eyes on every part of her backside.

***

Hunter needed to get back to the office, but his eyes were in control at the moment. He could not take them off Stephanie's long legs that went on forever or her fine sculptured ass. How could a *gluteus maximus* be so perfect and all on a five-seven frame. Her long, black, silk hair was in a braid that hung to the middle of her back and swayed as she walked, it only enhanced her beauty.

He had never met anyone as close to physical perfection as this woman walking out of their shop. My God, he had only dreamed of his ideal woman. Never in his life did he imagine he would ever meet a woman like that, but, oh man, was he wrong.

He did not need a distraction like this. He just needed to keep his mind on his family and work, that's all there was to it.

***

The following midmorning, half of Hunter's body was under the hood of his Toyota truck when he heard the sound of a Harley coming down his long driveway. Turning his head he saw Jake on Stephanie's bike, Pearl.

Jake slowed the bike to a stop next to Hunter.

"You know this is one cherry-looking bike and it rides nice too."

"Yeah and you should see the owner and you will know why. The bike fits her to a tee. The woman is definitely a looker."

"Well, I'll be a blue-nose gopher. You noticed another female besides Anne and Milly."

As soon as Jake made the comment he lifted his head up towards the sky as if he was looking for something.

Hunter followed Jake's gaze looking up at the cloudless sky.

"What the hell are you looking for?"

"I'm waiting for the pigs to fly by."

Jake was still looking up when he continued to talk.

"Remember a long time ago, I told you the day you become attracted to a woman is when pigs will fly? Well, I'm waiting to see one pass by."

Shaking his head, chuckling, Hunter remembered when Jake had said that. It was ages ago, before the bike shop was even a concept.

"Smart ass. I assume you already talked to her and now you're taking Pearl for a test drive."

"Yeah, I met Stephanie, I wouldn't mind taking that woman on a loooong personal test drive myself, if you know what I mean."

Jake wiggled his eyebrows up and down.

All Hunter had to do was look at him like he was going to drill him another asshole for Jake to realize that Hunter had claimed Stephanie for himself.

"I knew it! That woman has gotten to you. God, I feel I need to get down on my knees and start thanking the lord above."

"Oh shut the fuck up, Jake. She's a beautiful woman, big whoop. Nothing is going to happen between us, you know that. It's been years since I've have been interested in any other woman besides my main two."

"Well, you can talk all you want. As a matter of fact, go tell someone who would believe you, cause I don't. You know, dude, we go way back and I think I know you better than most, so no, I don't believe that bullshit you just spilled out. But I'm warning you, if her resume is as good as we think it is and she starts to work for us, you know she is going to be like honey to a bunch of god-blessed killer bees that stop by the shop. Even Spike might be interested."

Hunter glared at him ready to kill. Jake held his arms up in a surrender pose.

"All I'm saying is, you had better move fast, if you know what I mean."

With that said Jake drove off to finish his test drive.

Yeah, Hunter heard what Jake was saying, but he didn't want to think about it.

Hunter's reaction to the woman was not good. Stephanie

was throwing him. Good thing Jake hadn't been there when he first saw Stephanie, because the man would have witnessed his reaction to that beauty. Jake knew Hunter had never reacted like that to anybody. He had to keep his attraction toward that woman under control.

Hunter had to pull a Jake and not worry about it. If something happened between him and Stephanie, then it was meant to be. Even though there was nothing religious about Jake, he was a man of iron clad faith. Jake would say, "Let go, let God." There were no concerns for him; he would just give it to the big guy in the sky. Hunter was mentally patting himself on the back because he decided that's what he was going to do.

CHAPTER FIVE

A week and a half had passed and Stephanie was happy and feeling good that she had a new job. Stephanie walked into the small house she found through a local Realtor's rental list. What a difference this new job was compared to working in Silicon Valley. The pace was a lot slower than at the big corporate job and it was not as stressful. So far, so good.

When Stephanie was working as a successful graphic designer at a popular graphics company in San Jose, she was promoted to lead designer. To her, her life couldn't get any better. But it was a rude awakening when she found out the only reason she was promoted was because her boss thought her job duties involved letting that dick grab her ass whenever he felt like it.

Stephanie couldn't take his calculated and callous touch anymore, so she ended up punching him right in the face. It felt good to watch him land on his ass. She was not about to stay at that damn job any longer than she had to. No freaking way. So she quit. She had loved working for the company and loved working for everyone but him. When the CEO found out about her former boss's antics, she believed they would let him go. She could have filed a sexual harassment complaint, but she wanted to start anew somewhere else and she didn't want or need to hassle with a lawsuit. Also she knew he wasn't going to change his ways and would probably grab someone else's ass, but someday he would pay.

Stephanie was now enjoying her new job at PanHead Harley. She had felt at ease right away, as soon as she met Paula. It felt like she had known Paula forever. It was so comfortable talking to her. Paula easily could have been a sister or even a best friend, that's how natural it was between them. With Paula's long blond locks, which fell down to the middle of her back and her tiny, petite frame, some people would automatically take her for granted assuming that she was somehow fragile, but that couldn't have been further from the truth. This petite woman could hold her own. Steph had already seen Paula in action when she got pissed off. That little mama did not take any shit from anybody. That's exactly how Stephanie was also. Maybe that's why they clicked so much.

Paula's husband, Robert, a burly man with a full bushy beard, had sky blue eyes, that always had a twinkle in them, especially when he looked at the love of his life, Paula. He was one smitten man and proud of it. A nice guy all around and told a lot of good jokes. Robert and Jake were a crack-up to be with. Working at PanHead was a lot of fun and she fit in in such a short time. Which was good because it helped to keep her mind off Hunter.

Because both her and Hunter's office are at opposite ends she doesn't see Hunter much. Whenever one of them walks by the others office they would wave and that would be it. The last time she had spoken to Hunter was during the job interview. He had a lot of questions and she even noticed that there were times when his glance lasted a little longer than it normally should. But nonetheless she was offered the job and she couldn't be happier.

So far she had gotten along with all five of the PanHead's employees and from what Jake was saying, that in the near future they will be expanding the shop, tripling its size. Everyone was all jazzed about it. Jake already knew the people he wanted to hire. They were also going to work with San Lorenzo Valley High School, giving the students a space to learn and to work on motorcycles. This way Jake and Hunter would always have a choice to take the cream of the crop of the talented students.

Getting her second wind she decided she'd make herself one of her favorite dishes since it was so simple and fast to prepare. The ingredients consisted of sour dough loaf, butter, ground beef, ketchup, minced onions, chopped olives and mozzarella cheese and bake. Stephanie had just finished eating two pieces of her Hearty Hero when her phone rang. Putting the phone to her ear she could hear Paula yelling to Robert.

"Hey sweet-cakes, since you're getting a beer for yourself, will you throw me a soda please?"

"Hey, Paula, how's it going?"

"Hi, Steph, I forgot to tell you that once a year a group of us from the shop do a group run and ride down what we call "Scenic One," which is really "The Pacific Coast Highway.""

"The Pacific Coast Highway?"

"Yeah, we call it "Scenic One," it's easier to say. I wanted to know if you're game to join us?"

"When is this thing going to be happening?"

"Next Sunday. Since the shop will be closed it gives us an excuse to ride. What do ya say?"

"I don't have any plans, so that would be great, thanks. Where do we all meet?"

"We always meet at PanHead around eight a.m. and take it from there. OK?"

"Sounds good. I bet Jake, Spike and Rob will be the entertainment everyone, huh?"

"Oh yeah, that always happens. It will get even better once you meet the other two crazy guys.

"And who would they be?"

"They go by the names of Sam Collins and Jason Parks.You're going to have a ball. But I gotta go. See you Monday."

Enjoy your weekend off, my dear." Stephanie said bye and hung up.

***

As long as they were caught up on their orders, the shop usually would be closed on Sundays. If they ended up with a big order, those involved on the project would have to work. But Jake and Hunter made it a point to have the work orders done to make this annual ride. It supposedly had become a fun tradition for them all.

CHAPTER SIX

Jake planned to head out to the San Leandro in the East Bay to pick up various parts the shop had ordered. The owners were unable to deliver, as they usually did, due to a family emergency. They had called Jake to explain and he volunteered to head out there. They were old friends he and Hunter had known their family forever.

Once Hunter found out about Jake going to San Leandro, he knew he needed to go instead. This would be a nice break for his hormones. Every time he saw Stephanie, his body would react. He wanted a break.

Hunter surprised Jake and told him he'd be more than happy to go over the East Bay chopper shop and pick up what was needed. He decided he would stay a day or two to help out. Jake was more than happy to let Hunter do the pickup since two new orders had just arrived that day.

Hunter enjoyed his time there. It was good to visit and help his friends out. Kept his mind busy.

The day after Hunter arrived back home he was felt positive. Anne was doing great in school. Aunt Milly was busy with her writing and someone had just signed a lease on one of his commercial properties, which had recently vacant. Over the past ten years he had become a serious real estate investor and owned several buildings in Boulder Creek and even in Santa Cruz. Some of his commercial buildings were along Highway 9 and fortunate enough that they leased fast. This recent lease was for a building that had been empty for not even a month before he got a bite. And now he was a happy camper.

It didn't take long for the good feeling to turn into a predicament and didn't like the feeling one damn bit. He was still struggling when it came to that dark haired beauty who seemed to turn his libido upside down. His plan so far was to keep himself physically busy with his to-do list, which would help to keep his mind occupied without going into the Stephanie zone.

But now everything on his list had been completed and his brain went right back to picturing her the first day they met. Both he and Jake were blown away with Stephanie's portfolio; that woman was talented. So the two owners had a private powwow and decided not to hesitate. They offered her the job, not wanting to take the chance of this talented woman slipping out of their hands. Hunter had to laugh, he remembered how flabbergasted Stephanie was when she was offered the job. She absolutely freaked.

He realized where his mind was going again. He needed to change course and start making another one of his lists. This was getting ridiculous and he knew it. Hell, he knew the attraction for her was still there, but he kept telling himself that right now he couldn't deal with it. His family still needed him-financially, emotionally and physically. No way would he be able to get involved with anyone. No way, no how, as the saying went.

No sooner had he thought that then the next thought he heard was Jake telling him that he had taken stupidity to new heights. But really, who was he kidding? He'd been out of the relationship market for so long, he really didn't know how to relate to someone he was attracted to, unless it was just for a one-night stand. Even on those occasions he made sure he kept his distance. As a matter of fact, the only times he hooked up with someone for an overnight fling was when him and the guys went on a weekend trip. The last time that happened was when they rode their bikes to Nevada, eight months ago. So yeah, he was out of touch when it comes to relationships.

OK, enough of this bullshit and back to reality. Time to start another damn to-do list.

***

Jake walked into PanHead's office and noticed Hunter working on the computer, probably doing the bills.

"Hey, my man, I haven't seen you since you left for the East Bay, and that was what, four, five days ago? Where have you been hiding? Annnd… does this hiding have anything to do with the lovely and talented Stephanie?"

Shaking his head, without looking up from the computer.

"If I throw you a bone, will you leave?"

"Hey, damn, Hunt, that was funny, but I want to know, when did you grow a sense of humor? You know, it's quite an appealing trait for a man. Chicks love it."

Hunter looked up.

"And let me guess, you would know."

"Damn right I would know. FYI, from my experience with people, a sense of humor not only helps cuts their anxiety, it helps them to relax and it's also healing. It's an exercise you need to learn and practice."

Hunter humphed his response and replied.

"Well, all I can say is the only exercise you're getting is stretching the truth."

"Wow, man, that's two for the record book. We must be rubbing off on you. Or you're a poet and you just don't know it."

"OK, I give up. What is it you want so I can get back to the bills?"

"I came in here to get another pen. They seemed to be hiding from me. And speaking about hiding, what's with the invisible man act? Didn't know you for a coward. Man, if Collins and Parks knew about this disappearing act of yours, you wouldn't hear the end of it."

"Well, don't put your panties in a bind. It's not becoming. I've been busy with stuff that I have needed to do for a while. Being a coward has nothing to do with it."

Hunter was trying to throw an air of confidence as he spoke, not sure how it would be received.

"Yeah, buddy, just keep telling yourself that. So, the new girl, or I should say woman, has had no influence on this supposedly ongoing to-do list of yours?"

"What makes you think there's even a list, much less an ongoing one? I never said anything about a list to you!"

Jake nodded his head.

"No, you're right, you never said anything to me about a list, but both Anne and Aunt Milly did. And they're wondering what you're up to. They've never seen you so focused and determined to keep up with a damn list and your projects. Milly called me a few days ago, just out of concern. I knew what your problem was, but I played dumb, to cover for you."

"Well, at least the 'dumb' part wasn't too much of a stretch for you. Thanks."

"See, you did it again. There's some promise for you yet. Oh, by the way, were you planning on going with us riding down Scenic One, next Sunday?"

"Yeah, I'm going."

"Good, then make sure you don't forget to write that down on your sorry-ass-list."

Jake turned around and walked out.

"Smart-ass." Hunter mumbled.

CHAPTER SEVEN

God, Hunter thought, *all he needed was for his two other close friends, Collins and Parks, to hear what he's been up to and why; damn, he would never here the end of it.*

Jake and Hunter first got to know Sam Collins and Jason Parks when the two guys brought their Harleys to the shop ten years ago. They all got along so well they just started to hang out together, either working on their bikes or just riding.

Whenever the four guys went riding and made a pit stop, walking into a bar together, wearing their leathers, the women in the room stopped what they were doing to swarm the fab four. It was a pretty pitiful sight for the men who were left hanging.

Collins and Park had been best friends since high school. Collins, a well-known and successful architect for the last ten years, whereas Parks chose a profession in law enforcement working with the Santa Cruz County Sheriff Department for ten years, with two of those years as a sergeant homicide detective. These two guys were dedicated to five things and five things only. Their hogs, their family, their work, good food and loose women, not usually in that order.

Both Collins's and Parks's families lived out of the area in Orinda, CA. But they regularly kept in touch with all of them. Both sets of parents had lived in the same neighborhood since their sons were kids and the parents being best friends. When Collins and Parks were growing up, the families had many get-togethers. Once you witness a family get together you'd be able to see where both men acquired their sense of humor. Whenever the families came down for a visit, there would always be a get together, with the gang from the PanHead shop in attendance; they loved being with that crazy bunch yet close-knit of people. It felt good being around this close-knit group. For Hunter it brought back memories of his own family and how much they enjoyed being with each other.

It didn't matter where they were or what they were doing, when Hunter hung out with his three friends, he laughed so much his mouth and cheeks would hurt. There never was a dull moment with those three, not to mention the other crazy people he worked with. And next Sunday was probably going to be another one of those crazy days.

CHAPTER EIGHT

Stephanie was excited for the Scenic One ride. She'd heard how beautiful the ride along the coast was, but had never had a chance to ride it herself. Even though it was eight a.m. the weather felt like it was going to be perfect to ride.

She rode into the PanHead Shop on her beautiful, Pearl. As she slowed to a stop, when who did she see bent down on his knees, looking as fine as could be in his jeans, tweaking his bike, but Hunter himself. No sooner had both parties realized each other's presence than both pair of eyes had that "OH SHIT!" expression and don't think Jake didn't take notice.

Jake had plans for those two. This denial of their obvious attraction for each other had to stop. Being the friend that he was, he was going to do something about it. His plan involved lover boy Jason Parks and the "too hot to touch" Stephanie. If he was right, which he usually was when it came to his good friend Hunter, he knew he would get a reaction. If not, he would just have to kick some sense into him.

A little competition never hurt anybody and this would be exactly what Hunter needed. Just a little wake-up call back to reality. This was going to be an interesting day. Jake couldn't wait.

***

As soon as Stephanie got off her bike, Paula was there to give her a big hug. In these past few weeks the two women couldn't have gotten any closer. If Paula wasn't with her man, she was with Stephanie and Stephanie couldn't be happier. Since her parents lived in Colorado and her two brothers lived in the East Bay, she didn't see them as often as she would have liked, but now she had her Paula.

No sooner had Stephanie finished hugging Paula than the last of the group rode in. Stephanie had no idea who these two guys were, but they were eye candy for all with an XX chromosomes. She liked what see saw, but they didn't hold a candle to Mr. Tall, Dark and Silent. No matter, she needed Hunter's absence, since it made life so much easier to concentrate on other things, but she did wonder what he was like.

Everyone greeted the two newcomers with a slap on the back or a hug. Seemed like everyone liked these two guys. A few minutes later Jake steered the two newcomers towards her and introduced her as the newest member of the PanHead group to Sam Collins and Jason Parks.

Right away she noticed how Jason zeroed in on her and it wasn't too long after that she was laughing. If this was any indication of what the rest of the day was going to be like, she couldn't wait.

***

Seeing how Jason zoomed in on Stephanie, Hunter knew the day was going to be long and it was his own damn fault. For some damn reason he never thought she would join in on the ride. Maybe because he was so busy trying not to think of her that he forgot to even ask Jake.

He watched as Jason walked up to her and her bike and knew he should be thankful someone else was interested. But right now he was just plain pissed off and they hadn't even started riding yet.

Jake walked to his bike, which was in front of the group and gave a sharp whistle. He raised his arm, twirling it in a circular motion, indicating to start the engines. And what you heard was the beautiful rumble sound of eight Harley-Davidsons' motors turning over, – a sound only a Harley lover could appreciate.

***

Stephanie had always loved that patented low rumble sound. Where she grew up her father and brothers had Harleys and of course she had to keep up with them.

Stephanie turned around to see where Hunter was. He was at the rear, which suggested he was the most experienced rider in the group. When she turned back around, Jason, glided his bike into position next to her.

CHAPTER NINE

You couldn't have asked for a more perfect day to cruise the Pacific Coast Highway. Stephanie had heard so much about it from other biker friends, even her brothers, but she never had the chance to take the drive. Today was her lucky day. Riding along the ocean's edged, she glanced at the waves as they turned into each other, slapping against the large boulders and sending sprays of the ocean along the sand. This day couldn't have been any better.

***

Hunter was in his element as he was riding. The day was gorgeous and so was the backside view of the sexiest woman he had ever met. Damn, she looked good on her bike. No sooner had he thought that than he pictured Stephanie with her long shapely legs wrapped around him his waist... naked. Right away he knew those damn thoughts of his weren't going to get him anywhere, but they sure in the hell made his ride more enjoyable, even though his pants were tighter behind that zipper of his. He wasn't going to complain.

Their last stop before they turned back for home was in the town of Cambria. Hunter liked this town. When he was younger, he and his family rented a house across the street from the ocean, on Moonstone Beach Drive. Those were good times before he lost his parents.

The group had decided ahead of time to stop and eat lunch at the restaurant called Robin's. They liked how they could sit outside enjoying each other's company. It was a good thing Jake had called the restaurant ahead of time to inform them about their large group and to reserve a large table outside for them. The group started seating themselves at the table they were led to, although some of the riders were missing because of a needed run to the head (bathroom). Once Hunter walked in the dining are it was no surprise to him to see Stephanie sitting next to Paula, but what was a surprise was the seat that was next to her was still empty. Hunter thought Jason must still be in the head. *You snooze, you lose,* he thought and sat next to the woman of his fantasies.

Stephanie finished talking to Paula and thought it was probably Jason sitting next to her when she turned her head she was starring at the most beautiful light green eyes.

***

"Oh hey, Hunter, it's good to see again."

Stephanie did a quick glance of the table and noticed Jason taking a seat directly across from her.

She continued talking.

"Seems our schedules don't give us a chance to talk, so yeah, it's good to see you."

It was time for her to shut up, before she made a fool of herself.

"Well, it's good to see you too, Stephanie. How has Pearl been handling?"

"Oh, Hunter, she is one smooth ride. I sent a picture of her to both my brothers and they e-mailed me back telling me I did good and that she was a beauty. That meant a lot to me since my brothers are my heroes."

Hunter felt a pang of envy toward her brothers, but now he knew a way to warm her up to him.

"Tell me about your two heroes. Where are they now?" He noticed how she instantly relaxed. It was obvious talking about her family made her feel good.

"Well, I grew up wanting to be just like them. They were always so patient with me. Good thing, though, that I was a quick learner. When they played sports with their friends during the summer I learned how to play whatever they were playing and got good at it. When they were riding their dirt bikes, I wanted to learn too. When I was finally allowed to ride they had me start on a Honda 65cc, then went up to a Honda 85cc and finished off with my own Honda 150cc F."

Now Hunter understood her love to ride.

"How old were you when you first started on the 65?"

"I was seven, although I wanted to start when I was five years old, but my parents put a stop to that. They finally gave in, thanks to the nagging of my brothers. It was one of my birthday presents. Being told that my brothers were going to start teaching me to ride was one of the best birthday presents that I ever received. As you probably can tell, the three of us always did a lot together. We always had so much fun and we still do. It's just too bad we don't live closer to each other, but it's a lot better than living out-of-state from each other."

"Where do each of your brothers live and where do they work?"

"Well, Ryan is the oldest. He lives in Pleasanton and is a CHP motorcycle patrol officer. Brad he lives in Piedmont and has a veterinarian practice in Orinda. It seems the holidays are the only time when we can get together. I would love to get them to move over here."

CHAPTER TEN

Hunter couldn't have asked for a better time. Even though his conversation with Stephanie was constantly interrupted, they, along with everyone else were having fun razzing each other. They were laughing so much even the customers sitting at the other outdoor tables were also laughing. Either the laughing was contagious or they could hear what was being said.

Hunter decided no more avoiding Miss Pierce. After enjoying the short time of their one-on-one conversation, he was now looking forward to getting to know her even more. Now all he had to do was get rid of the yellow streak down his back.

***

Stephanie couldn't believe how easy it was to be around this group. She couldn't get over how much they laughed. Especially when Jake and Jason were giving each other a bad time about Jake's cooking abilities. Jake was bragging about how he had fixed one of his many lady friends an awesome dinner.

That was all Jason needed to hear.

"Listen Jake, I need to interrupt you for a second to give our newest member of the PanHead group an update."

Looking straight ahead at Stephanie, he leaned towards her with his elbows on the table. His face turned serious.

"Stephanie, when Jake starts rapping about his cooking you're just going to have to ignore it because he's such a bad cook he uses the smoke alarm as a timer."

It didn't take long for Jake to come back from Jason's remark and looked at Stephanie.

"Stephanie, my dear, you need to remember one thing about Jason and that is that he gives a lot of bull for somebody who hasn't got any cattle."

Right away Jason came back.

"But you know, you all have to agree that this man here" – he looked at Jake– "is a burger short of a Happy Meal. So just try to ignore him."

Once Jake stopped laughing he put his right hand to his heart and said to Jason.

"You're a good friend of mine, Jason and all I can say is, may your daughter's hair grow thick and abundant,…all over her face."

Again a roar, but Jason held up his arm to get the group to settle down.

"Yes, yes, I agree you are a funny man and I'm trying to see things from your point of view, but unfortunately I can't stick my head that far up my ass."

Hunter was laughing so hard and leaned farther back in his chair and started to fall over. Just in time Stephanie yanked him forward. Whereupon they just started to laugh again.

It was one great day had by all.

***

Lunch was over, stomachs content and full. Jake let the group know they had three hours of free time before they would all meet up at the Shell station for the ride back home. With that said they all started to split up. Hunter leaned into Stephanie's ear.

"I'd like to spend the next three hours with you, would you mind? I'm enjoying your company."

Stephanie felt like a damn teenager having the cutest boy in school paying attention to her. This was so pitiful, but having this hunk of a man wanting to be with her felt good. She had enjoyed talking to Hunter and felt comfortable with him. She wanted more of that. This was a first for her, and her stomach was doing somersaults of excitement. She did want to spend more time with him. The man not only looked like sex on a stick, but his smooth low voice was making her melt. Good God, the man did not realize how each word he was saying was making her body tingle all over.

"Sure, I'd like that. What would you like to do first?"

***

Boy, that was a loaded question. Hunter knew what he really wanted to do, but that sexual suggestion might not go over with her at the moment. He could only wish maybe someday. As soon as he leaned in closer to talk to her he could smell her fruity scent and it was driving him wild. He bet her body was covered with that scent, which only to turn his mind to those long legs of hers that went on forever. He pictured them wrapped around him. At the moment he needed to snap out of it.

"How about we walk on the beach for a while. Then we can check out all the shops till it's time to head out."

"OK, I'm game."

They were enjoying their time as they walked on the beach, getting to know each other even more, when they heard Hunter's name being called. They turn around to find Jake, Rob, and Paula walking towards them.

"Oh hey guys."

Hunter was surprised to see them.

Jake was shaking his head.

"Do you guys have any idea how far you have walked? The two of you are so busy flapping your jaws that you haven't been paying attention."

Stephanie realized their way was blocked by a massive wall of rock. They had walked all the way to the end of the beach.

"Oh my God."

Looking at Hunter.

"I didn't realized we walked so far."

"I didn't realize either."

He turned to look at everyone else.

"We might as well head by to town."

Jake shook his head.

"Good idea."

An hour had passed as they walked the soft sandy beach.

They spent the rest of the time walking around the town of Cambria, enjoying the cute shops. But now it was time to head back home. They all filled their tanks and started up their bikes, creating a thunderous roar in unison. Everyone around the area stopped and stared as they drove by. All in all it was a good day.

CHAPTER ELEVEN

As Hunter drove up to his house he saw Anne run out of Aunt Milly's house with the biggest smile. Not to far behind was his Aunt Milly, also wearing a big smile.

Hunter slowed to a stop. He held his arms open, knowing Anne was going to give him a hug.

"Hey Munchkin, what are you so excited about?"

"The people holding my horse called and said we can pick her up. Can we go now Hunter?"

"Sweetheart, the place would be closed by now. But why don't you get ready for school tomorrow and let me talk to Aunt Milly and see what they all had to say, OK?"

"OK, but I can't wait for tomorrow! Good night, Aunt Milly. Night Hunter, love you both."

Hunter looked at his aunt.

"What gives?"

Aunt Milly was still smiling.

"Apparently there were two more abused horses that came in. Since your horse has a home to go to, they acquired a special court order to approve you with ownership. You can pick up the horse up anytime tomorrow."

"Well that's good. But right now I've got a case of monkey butt and I need to stretch. Thanks for watching Anne."

"If I have told you once, I've told you twice, you don't need to thank me, I will always be here for the both of you. To be honest you're doing me the favor."

Aunt Milly was about to walk off when she remembered she had another topic to bring up.

"You know, Hunt, I've been, well, I mean Anne and I have been a little concerned for you. You have been so preoccupied with that damn list, making sure you're kept busy."

"How did you know the list was made to keep me busy?"

"Well, I asked Jake about you and he said, 'Well, the coward is trying to keep himself busy' but I don't think he caught on with what he said. But I have a feeling you are avoiding something, or should I say someone and I'm going to give you some advice young man, even if you don't want it. Hunter, you have devoted your life to Anne and I. We will never want you to be unhappy. Just recently Anne brought up the fact that she wishes you would find someone so you would have someone to make you happy and someone who would stick up for her whenever she got in trouble. So please, Hunter, give yourself a chance to be happy. Well, what I really mean is happier, because I know you are happy to be with us, but you are not complete. If anyone deserves that, it would be you Hunt."

She couldn't help but start to tear up.

Leaning against his bike, Hunter listened to what Aunt Milly was saying and it touched his heart. How could he not be happy with these two wonderful females in his life?

"Oh hey, come here and give me a hug. You know you guys are my life and I wouldn't want it any other way," he said, as he wiped the tear from her face.

"Yeah, we know that, but we want you to have more of a life than just with us. So no more being a coward, OK?"

"Well, it just so happens that I got to know the person I was avoiding and I think it's going to be OK."

"Just give yourself a chance, Hunter and quit hiding. You deserve all the positive the world has to offer."

Milly wiped her eyes, hugged Hunter and turned around, heading to her place.

I'll be damn.

Although he refused to admit he was hiding. Indisposed

was more like the correct word. *Yeah right!* Seemed like his subconscious knew the truth even though his conscious mind still didn't want to admit it.

He drove his bike into the garage and knew what he was going to do tomorrow.

***

Stephanie's desk was in the middle of her small office, facing the door, which allowed her to see whoever walked in, but she was so focused on what she was doing she didn't notice Hunter standing there.

He cleared his throat.

"Ummph," trying to get her attention.

She looked up shocked.

"Oh! I didn't even hear you much less see you. Hi there."

"Hi there yourself. You weren't kidding when you said that you love what you do so much that you get lost in it."

"Yeah, guilty. What's great about it is that the time goes by so fast, like now, I could have sworn it was about two o'clock, but looking at the clock, I see it's close to closing."

"I came by since you wanted me to tell you the latest news regarding the abused horse."

"You mean you heard from them already?"

Hunter explained what was going on.

"I wondered if you wanted to go with me to pick the filly up, so you could see for yourself."

"Oh my God, yes, I would love to go. What time are you planning on leaving?"

"Why don't we head out now?

"OK, but let me save my work and sign off. How about if I meet you at your truck."

"Sounds good, I'll see you in a few minutes."

Off Hunter went, relieved at how the conversation was turning out and how relaxed they were toward each other.

They decided to leave Stephanie's car at his place.

Once they were in his truck and doors closed, Hunter started the truck and drove off.

"Where is the horse being held?"

"In Felton."

"Really? Is that where the Santa Cruz SPCA is?"

"No, the SPCA is Santa Cruz. When they get over crowded some of the animals are taken to either Aptos or Felton."

"How did your sister react to this recent news?"

"Oh, she went crazy all right. She wanted to pick up the horse as soon as I arrived home. She made out a list of names again. I have a feeling she was so excited last night that she didn't get much sleep."

"Is she going to be able to go with us to pick up the filly?"

"She wanted to, but she had to go to her dance class. Our Aunt Milly took her for me. I think both of them are excited to see this horse. I had to warn them that the horse is severely malnourished. The filly's appearance will eventually change with the loving care we give her. But thank God tomorrow is Saturday, because I know Anne is going to want to sleep in the stall with the horse. I think I'm going to let her under the condition I sleep in the barn also."

"Boy, Hunter, Anne is going to flip out. I don't know if I mentioned it to you, but I was torn between going to vet school or being a graphic artist. Because I sure do love animals. I wish my brother lived over here so he could check out the horse for you, since he does pro bono work for special rescue animals."

CHAPTER TWELVE

It took about ten minutes to get to Felton. Hunter backed the trailer he was pulling into a long, wide driveway and parked it close to where the horses were kept.

When he and Stephanie got out of the truck, they saw a young girl pulling the malnourished horse towards them.

Hunter slowly walked to the filly, softly talking to her. He liked what he saw in the little one's eyes. They were more alert than the last time he saw her. The girl informed Hunter that once the horse was in the trailer he would need to go in the office to sign some papers to release the horse to him.

They settled the filly in the trailer. Hunter was about to head to the office when Stephanie gently touched his arm.

"Hunter, would you mind if I went in the trailer with the filly while you're in the office, just to be with the horse?"

She still couldn't get over how the energy between the two of them was so strong. This had never happened to her and it was confusing. She didn't know how to react.

She had dated numerous men, but none of them made her insides do somersaults just by being near them. And she had not wanted to be intimate with anyone-until Hunter. Yes, you read right she was virgin. She was twenty eight years old and a god-blessed virgin. She hadn't planned this. It was just that she'd been so focused on her career that she had no interest, not one, in getting involved with a man. It was too bad that it had taken her so long to get any kind of reaction from a man.

Now she didn't know what to do. But to be honest, that wasn't the only reason. Living with two horndogs for brothers, seeing how they went through their women as often as they changed their underwear,– that was not for her. She realized she never wanted the come-and-go type of man.

***

Man, being this close to Stephanie was throwing his hormones off kilter.

"Sure, go ahead and visit," Hunter replied. "Just make sure you talk softly with her until she gets more comfortable with all of us."

As he was talking his hand casually covered her hand that still held on to his arm.

"Jesus, your hand is soft."

He realized he had spoken out loud, but it was too late since she had heard what he said; he should have kept his damn mouth shut. God, sometimes he was such a idiot.

She reacted fast and pulled away.

Who would have known that this woman would make him ramrod stiff whenever he saw her?

"OK, I'll see you in a bit."

He turned around and walked to the office.

***

Stephanie walked to the trailer, but before she went in, she started to talk to the filly in a soft tone. She stood there for about five minutes before she even attempted to get up in the trailer. Once she was in her soft voice never changed its tone. When Stephanie was standing next to the filly the horse turned its head toward her as she kept rubbing the filly's neck while she talked.

My God, this poor horse. How is it possible it's to still be alive? The filly was one lucky horse. Stephanie wasn't sure if the horse's hair was a lighter brown or dark brown, since the horses coat was filthy. It looked like they tried to wipe the horse down with a wet cloth and she bet with the lack of volunteers, the horses were unable to get washed. The hair on the horse reminded Stephanie of that shaggy mutt of a dog in the old movie called "Benji," that she and her mother loved to watch when she was a young girl. The little filly's hair did not have the smooth look like most horses, but was a bit longer and coarser.

She was shocked to see that the rib bones and hips were protruding out. This horse should not be alive.

***

Hunter finished signing the papers and headed back to the trailer, happy that the horse was officially Anne's now. He noticed that Stephanie wasn't sitting in the truck; she must still be with the horse. He walked to the back of the trailer. The doors were wide open. He saw Steph's hand rubbing the horse's back, nice and slow and heard her softly talking to the filly. He had no idea what she was saying, but the horse's head was bowed as it leaned against Stephanie's head. Whatever Stephanie was saying, the horse was feeling it.

Stephanie heard someone stepping in the trailer and knew Hunter was there. She rubbed the horse one last time and gave it a quick kiss. Turning toward Hunter, she looked in his eyes and he could tell she had been crying for the horse. That just added another point in her favor.

They walked to the truck without saying a word. Once the truck doors were closed Stephanie spoke.

"I do not understand how people could treat each other like shit, much less a defenseless animal. God, Hunter, when I see any type of injustice, I see red. Right now I want to go beat the crap, out of the person who did that to that darling of a horse."

Hunter couldn't help but melt. He completely understood what she meant. He reached for her hand and just held it.

"We both had the same reaction. But now the horse is safe and will be loved for the rest of her life. She is one of the lucky ones."

He couldn't get over how the simple act of holding her hand was not only appreciated, by her glance, but a reminder of the positive charge these two have between each of them.

Hunter started to tell her about his own horse, Blaze, who also was a rescue horse that Anne loved. Thank God, Blaze was not abused like this filly had been. The former owner of Blaze had died and when Hunter heard about it he wanted to adopt it.

It didn't take them long to get back to his place.

CHAPTER THIRTEEN

"Would you like to meet my sister and aunt? I mentioned to them last night that I was going to see if you wanted to go with me to pick up the horse. Anne wanted me to bring you over so she could meet you and Aunt Milly agreed. And when I was getting ready to walk out the door Aunt Mil yelled to make sure you stayed for dinner. So would you mind staying over for dinner?"

"Oh my goodness, I would love to meet them and yes, I would be happy to stay for dinner. I really want to see Anne's reaction when her horse finally comes home. From what you've told me about Anne, I think that horse is going to fall in love with her."

Hunter was holding her hand. He couldn't let it go. It just felt so…, good.

"Yeah, you're right. But I think the horse already made a new friend. I wish I had a camera, Stephanie, the way the horse was leaning toward you. The horse was eating up all the love you were giving it. It was a touching sight."

While Hunter was talking Stephanie was looking at their hands entwined. She appreciated what he said and gave him a beautiful smile.

"Thank you, Hunter. That was exactly what I was feeling for the horse. It was special moment for me too."

***

It was already dark outside when Hunter turned his truck

into the driveway. In the barn where all the lights were on and you could see Anne jumping up and down, with Aunt Milly next to her, laughing. Hunter backed the trailer in towards the barn.

Running towards Hunter, Anne leaped on her brother giving him a big hug.

"Thank you, Hunter, for letting me keep Patches. I promise to be responsible and to love her."

"You're welcome, sweetheart, I want you to meet Stephanie Pierce. She is the new designer for our shop. She has a lot of cool drawings you should see."

Anne knew she was going to like Stephanie, she felt it.

"Nice to meet you Stephanie. I'm glad Hunter brought you by. Are you staying for dinner?"

"Nice to meet you too, Anne. I would love to have dinner with all of you."

Hunter then introduced his aunt.

"This woman here is Aunt Milly, who has always been there for the two of us."

Aunt Milly looking lovingly at her nephew.

"And I always will Hunter. I'm so glad to meet you, Stephanie. He forgot to mention how gorgeous you are. And it's going to be nice to have some company."

Stephanie blushed.

"Well, thank you, I'm looking forward to dinner and getting to know all of you."

As Stephanie said that her eyes went directly to Hunter's. He got the hint was also looking forward to getting to know her even more.

Anne walked to the trailer, anxiously waiting for her aunt and Stephanie to finish with the introductions.

"Hunter, come on. I want to see Patches."

"OK, let's do it. By the way, perfect name, sweetheart."

He opened the trailer doors and you could hear him talking to the horse softly for a few minutes. Then he gently guided her backwards down the ramp until she was on the ground.

Hunter looked at Anne.

"OK, Anne, I want you to walk slowly toward Patches with no sudden movements. Just rub her first and introduce yourself talking as softly as you can."

Anne slowly walked toward Patches while calmly soothing the horse with her voice. It was so obvious how these two young ones instantly connected. Patches leaned her head as close as she could to keep Anne rubbing. Anne looked at Hunter with tears running down her face.

"Oh, Hunter, how could anyone have been so cruel to her?"

Not needing an answer Anne put her arms around Patches' neck saying.

"Don't worry, my Patches. Pretty soon you are going to be beautiful and I promise you, you will always be loved."

It was as if the horse knew what Anne was saying. She neighed while bobbing her head up and down, as weak as she was.

Hunter put his arm around Anne.

"Anne honey, we need to get her fed and warm."

"I don't want to leave her tonight, Hunt."

"I know, baby. That's why you and I are sleeping in here tonight."

You could tell that she wanted to jump up and down, but she held back because of the horse. She walked over to Hunter and gave him one of her tight hugs.

"Thank you. This way we can give Blaze attention too. Hunter, you're the best."

"While I'm getting Patches fed and comfortable, why don't you go get our sleeping bags and pillows."

"OK," and off she went.

Aunt Milly wiped her eyes.

"I'm going to finish getting dinner ready and put it on the table, so make sure you guys don't take too long."

She walked off.

Holding Kleenex, Stephanie also wiped her eyes.

"God, Hunter, she touched my heart."

"Yeah, she touched mine too."

***

Hunter grabbed a blanket and covered Patches. He picked up the bucket and fed her the amount of grain he had been instructed to feed her; since the horse was so malnourished she should not eat a lot at first. But each day he would gradually increase the amount of her food intake.

While the horse was eating, Stephanie kept rubbing her.

"You ready?"

Hunter closed the barn door behind them.

"Yeah, let's go."

They left the barn when Stephanie was surprised when he reached for her hand, without thought. It felt good being with him. This was definitely a first.

No sooner had they walked through the door to the house when Anne walked in the living room carry two sleeping bags and two pillows. She was already in her pajamas and robe with her slippers on.

"I'm so excited, Hunter."

"I don't blame you, sweetheart. But what I also need to do before tomorrow is write down a feeding schedule for Patches, per the doctor's instructions. Also, make sure you bring your camera with you tonight so we can have photos of Patches as we keep track of her progress each week, OK?"

"Yeah, that's a good idea. I'll go get it now."

Stephanie looked at Hunter.

"I'm going to see if your aunt needs any help."

Stephanie was about to leave when he stopped her. Hunter reached out and put a hand on her cheek and started to gently rubbed his thumb along her luscious lower lip.

"OK, I'll be in there in a few minutes. I need to clean up."

She didn't know how to react to that, so she smiled and self-consciously looked down and walked toward the kitchen.

Hunter couldn't take his eyes off Stephanie. He was surprised he caught what was an insecure reaction. She always carried herself in confidence. He doesn't know her good enough, yet, to know what that reaction was.

And since when did he start getting so brave? He almost shit himself when he realized he was rubbing her lower lip and what a lip that was. It was obvious his body had a mind of it's own. If he had thought about it he would have hesitated until it was too late. But now, he was glad that he did. So he hurried into his bathroom, took a quick shower and went to see what their guest was doing.

***

Stephanie walked in the kitchen and Milly made her feel comfortable right away. The more Milly talked, the more relaxed she felt. She loved Milly's sense of humor. But what surprised her was when out of the blue Milly brought up the topic of Hunter.

"Now I can understand why Hunter was staying occupied for the last few weeks."

Then Milly looked at the door, to make sure Hunter wasn't going to walk in.

"This is a first for him."

Stephanie had no idea what she was talking about.

"I don't understand. What do you mean?"

She heard Hunter walking toward the kitchen. She would not get her question answered quite yet.

"Auntie, do you want me to help with the drinks and put them on the table?"

"Please. Thanks Hunt."

While Hunter took care of the drinks, Stephanie finished cutting up the carrots and put them in the salad.

"Would you like me to put the salad on the table?"

"That would be great, thanks Steph."

The four of them sat down. They enjoyed each other's company. When they had finished, Anne looked up from her now empty plate with a serious look on her face and looked Stephanie.

"I really like you Stephanie, will you be my brothers girlfriend?"

Stephanie wasn't sure who started choking on their food first. She was so stunned she didn't know what to say. Aunt Milly saved them.

"Anne, that type of question should not be asked by you.

This is between your brother and Stephanie."

"I know, but I really like Stephanie and I want to keep seeing her. I'm afraid Hunter will start writing a new list and then nothing will happen."

Aunt Milly started to laugh. Hunter was too preoccupied choking on his food. Stephanie just looked confused as she was hitting Hunter on his back.

Once everyone was settled Aunt Milly looked to Anne.

"It looks like you're done eating. Why don't we leave these two people alone? And how about if I go with you, after you brush your teeth and we'll wait for Hunter in the barn, what do you say?"

"OK, auntie, that would be great."

Anne got up and walked around the table and gave Stephanie a big hug. And whispered in her ear.

"Please come back."

Then she released Stephanie and waved bye to her.

CHAPTER FOURTEEN

Once Anne and Milly left, Stephanie felt nothing but awkward. By the looks of Hunter he didn't know what the hell to say either.

"Ahhh, sorry about that, Stephanie. I hope she didn't embarrass you too much."

"Well, to be honest, I'm still trying to decide what all she was saying means."

"Well, I have an idea. Since you have tomorrow off, would you go out with me? That way I will be able to explain everything to you."

"Ah, sure. OK, what time?"

"How about if I pick you up at your place at 6 p.m? I want to start early to be able to spend some time with you. Why don't you write down your address and phone number on the tablet that's on the end table over there?"

Hunter gestured his chin toward the end table.

"I would have gotten it eventually from your records, but I was too blown away when I got the news about the horse."

"No, no, that's fine, I don't mind giving it to you."

She walked to the end table and wrote down her phone number and address.

"Maybe I should head for home."

She was now glad that she had listened to Hunter and left her car at his place when they went to pick up the horse.

Hunter took her hand.

"I'll walk you to the car."

Stephanie grabbed her purse.

"I want to thank you for inviting me over to meet your family. They both are wonderful. I could get attached to Anne. There's something special about her."

Hunter lifted her hand to his lips.

"My aunt and sis were both excited to meet you and I could tell they liked you a lot, also."

When they reached the car Stephanie turned to look at Hunter. He leaned over and gave her the most unbelievable kiss. Just by that kiss she understood what was was missing with the other guys she had kissed. Passion. Man, this guy had it in spades and she wanted more.

When the kiss was finished, he looked in her eyes.

"I have been wanting to do that since day one of meeting you. Before you start asking questions I will explain everything tomorrow night."

He gave her a quick kiss on her forehead.

"See you tomorrow."

He turned around and walked away heading for the barn.

Stephanie was flabbergasted. She couldn't stop herself from staring as she watched him. She surprised herself when she heard a moan coming from her throat. *God, that guy is just nothing but fine.* Her eyes were stuck staring at his backside - well to be more specific, a butt that should be bronzed. How could plain blue jeans bring out someone's attributes? Good God, they sure did on him. Just looking at it made her want to softly rub that rounded butt up and down along the curve then give it a good squeeze. It was confusing how one man could get such a reaction from her. If she didn't stop she would start drooling...again. She needed to be gone, like now. She got in the car and left for home.

***

The following morning Hunter woke up from a sound sleep feeling great; even though it was only a three-hour sound sleep, he felt good. He had a good idea why. He dreamed of her. Yes, Stephanie and it was one of the most erotic dreams he'd ever had, so erotic it was the most sated sleep he's had since he met her.

He realized now he had wasted all this time working on his to-do list, when he could have been with Stephanie. He now admits what he pulled was an act of avoidance from Stephanie. This only caused frustration and denial, which only made him physically exhausted, not to mention giving him the pleasurable, but frustrating dreams he had of Stephanie.

Last night watching Anne, she was in seventh heaven showering Patches with love. That little filly sucked all up all the attention she was receiving. The two of them are going to be good for each other.

Hunter was in his truck ready to leave for Stephanie's place. He was backing out when he heard and saw Anne yelling his name, running from the barn. He stopped the truck and waited for her.

"Hunter, have fun tonight. And don't forget to tell Stephanie to come back. OK? I really like her."

"I promise I'll bring Stephanie back to see you guys. She also told me she would like to get to know you more."

With a big smile, Anne jumped up and kissed Hunter's arm that was sticking out of the window and ran off.

"Thanks Hunt. Bye."

Hunter arrived and parked his truck in front of Stephanie's place. His stomach reacted in a way he had never felt before, as if he had butterflies in his stomach dancing a jig. Damn, this was a first for him in many ways. He couldn't remember the last time he was ever out on a date. A one-night stand, yeah, but that would not count as a date, so no, it had been a long while. He knew he wanted to get to know Stephanie even more so he would have to suck it up. Not going to take the chance of Jason becoming her knight in shining armor. Not going to happen.

***

Stephanie was excited for her date with Hunter. She had heard stories from Paula and even Jake that this man only took time out for two women and two women only. She could understand why. They were both wonderful. She hoped she would be able to get to know Milly and Anne even more.

She remembered how Hunter's eyes sparkled with pride when Anne said the horse's new name. The name Patches was perfect given what that poor horse had gone through.

But even though Stephanie was looking forward for her date, a part of her was a little nervous. She knew Hunter was going to open up to her, she just didn't know how much.

At the moment she was having trouble with her long dark hair. It was getting too long, so she was trying to wear it up, but her hair was not cooperating. It was always so much easier to wear her hair in a braid. She loved her braid and always thought it was pretty, but most importantly her braid was easy to deal with, especially if she needed to jump on her bike. Tonight, it looked like she had no choice and just to wear it down. She had just finished brushing her bangs when the doorbell rang. She took a deep breath and walked towards the front door.

When Stephanie opened the door, Hunter just stood there staring. Since he'd known her, he had never seen her without a braid. And my God, she looked gorgeous.

"Damn, Stephanie, you're beautiful. I've never seen your hair down like that. You look great."

Stephanie was also stomped. There stood Hunter in his eye-popping jeans, wearing a white button-down shirt and a worn dark brown leather jacket. He looked scrumptious.

"Thank you. You clean up pretty good yourself. Come on in, I need to turn on the light on my nightstand before we go."

When Stephanie came back to the small foyer, she noticed Hunter had moved into the living room and was looking at her family pictures on the wall.

"You have a good-looking family, Steph and you look like you love the hell out of all of them. I can tell just by looking at these pictures. And I also remember how you talked about your brothers in Cambria. Your love for them was very obvious."

"God, that was so much fun. I don't think I ever laughed so

much and so hard."

"Well, prepare yourself because that happens whenever any of those guys are around. Not only Jake and Jason – Rob, Spike and Collins are not too far behind in the humor department. If you were the depressed type those people would be great to have around. You'd be unable to stay depressed with any of those guys."

"Thanks for the warning. Where did you want to go tonight?"

"Well, I'm going to leave that up to you because I have no idea what your taste is for dining. For example, there's Scopazzi's, Restaurant. One of the local restaurant here in Boulder Creek, or there's the fancier one like, Shadowbrook, in Capitola. I'm not sure what you like."

"Well, what I'm going to tell you really pisses my family off, because they all like dressing up when they go out to a nice restaurants, but my idea of going out to eat is fast food. One of my favorites is McDonalds. I love the Big Mac's. I just don't have them that often."

"Well, I'll be damned. You're a girl after my own heart. Although fast food is not my favorite, I could do without dressing up for dinner, Santa Cruz Diner or Chili's are casual and I really like the food at both places. I especially like Red Robin, but there isn't one in Santa Cruz County. Which one do you want to go to?"

"Oh man, I love Red Robin restaurants. Since I moved here, Paula has taken me to the Santa Cruz Diner and I've eaten at Chili's, I love both places too. But let's go to the Santa Cruz Diner, that would be perfect."

"Santa Cruz Diner it is."

"Did you know that the Santa Cruz Diner was featured on some food network program? I can't remember the name of it, but the young chef has that platinum blond spiky hair. Paula told me that the Santa Cruz Diner is always busy, but that doesn't bother me if it doesn't bother you."

CHAPTER FIFTEEN

It had been a while since Hunter ate at Santa Cruz Diner and was looking forward to spending time with Stephanie. Opening the diners door, the aroma of sauté onions brought back memories of the place. He remembered the they had a variety of food on the menu and he enjoyed his meals. He always tried something different and was never disappointed.

The L-shape restaurant was always busy. There was nothing fancy about the place. Inside, a variety of pictures, odds and ends, scattered around, hung on the walls.

The place was set up with the longer part of the restaurant parallel with Ocean street. That side had all booths with windows. Where as the short side had booths along the windows and on opposite side of the wall, some booths and table and chairs in the middle of the floor.

Their wait at the restaurant wasn't long and were seated in the back corner, of the short side, away from the majority of movement.

Stephanie was anxious for what Hunter had to tell her.

"You know, Hunter, I'm little nervous, not sure what you wanted to talk to me about."

Sitting across from Stephanie, he reached out for her hands, which were folded on the table.

"I want to get to know you more. I am very attracted to you and want to see where it takes us. Although I must admit I'm pretty rusty on this dating or even being interested in someone. So if I somehow screw up, give me a little break, OK?"

That made Stephanie laugh.

"OK, on one condition."

"Oh-oh, what's the condition?"

"Well, I haven't been out on many dates either and it's not about being rusty. My problem is that I just don't know what I'm supposed to do or how to act."

Hunter was silent just looking at Stephanie.

"OK, Hunter, now you're making me nervous. Did I say something wrong?"

He laughed.

"Sorry, Steph. I figured with your looks you had dated quite often. So your saying you don't know how to act on a date shocked me. How in the world can that be?"

"Well, to be honest, the dates that I had, I knew there was nothing between those guys and me. So there was no point in continuing to go out with them. I just lost interest and focused on my graphic design classes. My brothers couldn't have been happier. Because they would want to meet 'em and beat 'em anyway."

Hunter had to laugh.

"Well, I can understand where they're coming from. There's is no one good enough for their sister and they're going to prove it. I'll probably be the same way when Anne gets old enough to start dating. It's like a man's right of passage when he has a sister. It's just automatic."

The evening was turning out great for both of them. Hunter told Stephanie how his parents died, one right after the other when Anne was only five years old. His mother had pancreatic cancer and she died four months from when she was diagnosed, leaving the family, shattered. Especially his father who was devastated that he died three months later. He was physically fit and it was believed he died of a broken heart. He just lost his will to live when the love of his life died. Hunter noticed how Stephanie's eyes teared up.

"Now tell me about your family."

Stephanie started to tell Hunter about her family. Her father and mother who were always laughing and were devoted to each other. Both loved to ride the Harley, ski, and hike, so once the kids grew up they left their Palo Alto home and moved to Colorado Springs. The family would take turns every Christmas/New Year holiday, either the kids flying to Colorado or the parents coming to California. It really didn't matter where they were; they always had fun. It was their father who had turned the boys on to Harley's. He and their mom were always riding when they could and he still owned his chopper.

"Hunter, tell me how you got to know Jake and all those other crazy guys. You all seem to get along with each other so well."

"Oh, it was crazy. I met Jake in high school in auto shop, which was a prerequisite before you could take motorcycle shop. Some of the guys in my class stayed with auto shop while others, like Jake and I, went to cycle shop.

Jake was easy to get along with. He treated everyone as a friend and was liked by everyone. He was pretty popular, especially with the girls."

"What about you, Hunter, what were you like then?"

"Nothing like Jake. I was a little bit more serious and liked to stay in the background. I avoided attention and still do. But it's easy for Jake and easy to be with Jake. I have always enjoyed and respected him. He may be a smart ass, but he's really a good guy. Just don't let him know I said that. He was always the one who stuck up for someone being victimized by a bully. That is something that still pisses him off and that's when his normally good nature leaves him. He will not tolerate someone being picked on. His little brother has a lot to do with how he feels about bullies. But that's a story for another time."

Hunter pushed his plate away. He leaned back on the cushioned booth with his stomach full and a satisfied look on him.

"Let me give you an example on Jake's reaction to bullies.

Jake and I were on our lunch break in high school and we were walking past the gym when he saw this kid he'd befriended the prior year. The kid, Mike, was a sophomore, while we were juniors. Jake got to know him since he volunteered, for extra credit, to help some of the special-needs kids. Well, this kid was one of his assignments and the two of them had become close. Anyway, when we walked around the corner of the gym, we saw the kid up against the wall with four guys in a semicircle around Mike, blocking him from getting away. One of the guys kept pushing him and laughing, calling him names. Well, Jake, being Jake, rushed over, grabbed the guy and stood between the kid and the idiot. He glanced at Mike to make sure there were no marks on him. All he noticed was that the kid was scared. He quickly put his hand on the Mike's shoulder to comfort him, then turned and looked at the idiot and said, 'From what I see, you need three of your buddies to protect you while you're talking to my man, Mike here, why is that?'

The idiot thought he had the edge and said, 'Hey, man, what the fuck is it to you? Why don't you go play with yourself and leave us alone with the retard?'

Hunter started to laugh.

"I knew Jake well enough to know he was in a slow burn and ready to break."

Stephanie was so focused on what Hunter was saying.

"Well, what happened?"

"Jake calmly looked at the idiot's three friends, one at a time and said." 'You know, your friend here is depriving a village somewhere of its idiot and it's not a good idea to be with him.' The three guys were laughing their heads off, while the idiot was giving them his bad ass look, or so he thought. About fifteen seconds later the laughing guys finally got themselves under control. The idiot still needed to somehow recover what was left of his pride to reply, 'What's it to you? This guy probably can't even count to ten.'

That last remark did it, Jake was pissed and said to the guy, 'Yeah well, you couldn't count to twenty-one if you were barefoot and without pants.' Then Jake punched him in the face and put his arm around Mike and we walked away."

"Did Jake get sent to the dean?"

"Nope, no one reported him. Even the idiots friends didn't do anything."

"Well, I liked Jake prior to your story, but now I think the guy is great. I'm proud of him."

"Yeah, like I said, a good guy."

"You know, Hunter, this has been a fun night. To be honest, I didn't know what to expect."

"Yeah, but I want more."

He reached out for her hand.

"A lot more."

Stephanie's face turned red. She looked down, but her hands stayed entwined with Hunter's.

"You know, you look cute when you blush."

"Well, don't get use to it. I seldom blush."

"We'll see about that. Have you ever been to the Beach Boardwalk on Friday nights?"

"No, but I've been wanting to go to those free concerts they have on Fridays. Did you want to go?"

"Yeah, Eddie Money is going to be there tonight, but I just want to make sure you liked him too."

"Oh, I love him. He's one of my grandmothers favorites with my mom liking his music. She used to play his albums a lot when we were growing up. Let's go."

"Sounds good."

They sat on the beach as they watched the show. When it was over, they decided go to take advantage of the warm evening and go for a walk farther down the beach. It was easy to talk to her. The longer Hunter was with her, the more he wanted her and the braver he was getting.

CHAPTER SIXTEEN

He parked his truck in front of her small, 900 square foot house. Once his car was in park he leaned in to Stephanie and softly rubbed her lower lip.

"God, I want you, Stephanie and I want to stay overnight with you too. I know I'm rushing it, but I don't want to control myself. All I could think about tonight was my hands all over your body."

"Come inside, Hunter."

"Yeah, that's what I want to do too."

"No, Hunter, I meant come inside the house, you perv," she said, laughing.

"I tell ya, I'm unable to think of anything else, so let's just go inside."

As soon as they were inside the house, Hunter locked the front door, turned around, and pulled Stephanie against his chest.

"Do you have any plans tomorrow?"

Stephanie looked in his eyes.

"Yeah, as a matter of fact I do."

Disappointed Hunter looked at her.

"What do you have to do?"

"Well, I plan on staying in bed all day with you."

As soon as she said that, Hunter lifted her up. She wrapped her legs around him.

"Which way to your room?"

"Down the hall and the door on the left."

In the bedroom Hunter pulled Stephanie's top off in a single motion and started leaving tender trails of kisses from her neck down to her chest. He gave his full attention to her breasts, sucking, kissing, licking.

He dreamed of this. Hunter loved how Stephanie's long legs wrapped around his waist when they flopped on the mattress. The two of them were in a panic mode, taking each other's clothes off. As Stephanie's hair fell on his face, the fruity scent drove him crazy. His passionate feelings for Stephanie was throwing him for a loop. How could he have gone so long and not felt such a powerful pull for one woman? Now, though, he didn't care, he wanted her. *Mine.*

***

Stephanie was going crazy and she wanted more. Never in her life had she felt like this for any guy, but she did for Hunter. She couldn't get his clothes off fast enough. She wanted him in her and now. She had dreamt of this for awhile, but now that it was happening it was blowing her mind. On top of Hunter, Stephanie finally got the last stitch of clothing off of him. She started to leaned back as she straddled him, only to push herself farther down Hunter's thigh. Stephanie took her time as she gazed at every inch of that magnificent body of his.

"You keep looking at me that way, sweetheart and I'm going to burst like a fourteen year old. I've been fighting this since I've met you, but not anymore. Grab my pants, baby and get me a condom that's in one of the back pockets."

Stephanie was busy kissing and nipping at his chest when she stopped what she was doing and leaned back again to look at him, giving him the sexiest closed mouth smile he could manage. Before she got up to get the condom she scooted a little further back to expose his throbbing organ, which was definitely ready to play. She gently cupped his balls, sliding her hand back and forth, then gently squeezed them. Her hand slid upwards and started to slide up and down in slow motion. Only to increase tempo while she gently squeezed him, along with rubbing them in a circular motion. She looked down, enjoying the sight, then lifted her eyes to gaze into Hunter's eyes.

"Baby,...I'm not ... going to be... able to...hold on."

Since when did she get so brave? But damn, she felt naughty and she liked it, especially with Hunter. She just hoped she was doing everything right. Watching some x-rated movies helped when she was home alone, thanks to Comcast On-Demand. But man, this man was beautiful, with his pre-climactic expression.

"Then come."

That did it, Hunter burst spraying on his stomach.

"God, Hunter, you're just too hot for your own good."

Seconds later Hunter was getting hard again. She knew she had to hurry and get the condom. She found his jeans and took it from his pocket.

***

Hunter's eyes devoured Stephanie.

"Come here."

She leaned over and gave him a hungry kiss.

Grabbing the condom from her.

"I want you now, Steph."

Hunter was having a hard time trying to put the condom on since his hands were shaking. Another first for him. Stephanie took the condom and slowly slid the rubber down, only to end up cupping his balls.

"Oh no, you don't."

He grabbed her by the waist and switched positions, with him now on top of her.

"God, I need to be in you, right now."

He knew what she wanted and aligned himself to her as he slowly started to enter her. He gently pushed himself in far enough and was seconds away from pushing harder when he felt the thin barrier and realized she was a virgin. All of a sudden he pulled out.

He stopped what he was doing and pushed his arms to raise himself up. He stretched his arms up on each side of her head and looked at Stephanie.

"How in the hell can you still be a virgin? Steph, I almost un-virgined you."

Stephanie had to laugh.

"Yeah, well, that was the point."

"Stephanie, are you kidding me? How could you still be a virgin? You are so damn irresistible to the opposite sex. How were you able to keep them off you?"

"Hunter, I don't want you to think that you can hurt me. From what I've read, slight discomfort is to be expected when you are a virgin. The pain should only last for a second, that's all."

"Baby, how can that be? How were you ever able to hold back so long?" He may have been surprised, but it sure made him feel damn good that she chose him to give up her virginity.

"Well, at first my brothers scared the hell out of any guy that looked at me twice throughout my school years. Even though they were older than me somehow, they knew who I was interested in or who was interested in me and they pretty much stopped it. I'm guessing they ended up talking to whoever was their target. It really didn't bother me since I did everything with my brothers. They even let me play sports with them and their friends. Tomboy, was my middle name. God, I loved it. As you're probably finding out I'm not your typical girl or woman. I never was, growing up with the two brothers of mine. I loved being treated like one of the guys.

"Yeah, but still, didn't you date in college?"

"Nope. Had no interest. I was so focused on my graphic design career that it took up most of my attention."

"But how could you not be approached by some interested guy?"

"Oh, that was easy. I just told whoever asked me out that I didn't think my boyfriend would approve. It was that simple."

Stephanie wrapped her arms around Hunter's neck.

"Besides this was my choice. I wanted it to be special when I finally made love and that person just so happens to be you."

"Wow, I just realized that I'm one lucky son of a bitch."

"Yeah, you are. Now can we finish what you had started?"

"Sure, hon, but now that I know, I'm hesitant."

"Hunter, I understand, but you're going to have to realize this is just part of a woman's anatomy, so don't worry."

"Damn, I don't know, maybe we should wait for a little bit."

"Yeah and maybe we should wait for pigs to fly?"

"Funny you should say that."

"Hunter, what I'm saying is a big fat *no*, we are not waiting, I have made my choice and now that you have given me a taste of things to come, I want more. But to be honest and up front, please don't expect me to know what the hell I'm doing. I just don't want to disappoint you."

Stephanie pulled a Hunter and rolled the both of them over, where she was now on top of him again.

She started to slowly rub her body against Hunter's long erection, moving up and down, side to side. His erection came back to life. She was now slowing moving her body with his hardness getting harder with each stroke.

Stephanie looked in his eyes.

"Now that's what I'm talking about."

"Honey, for a virgin who is not quite sure if you're doing it right,Hunter lowered his head close enough into Stephanie's ear, – you are."

***

It didn't take long for the fire to ignite again between the two of them. Their passion for each other was obvious. It seemed like they couldn't get enough of each other. One on one, skin to skin, just wasn't enough. If there was a way to get closer they would have found it.

Hunter was so turned on that he completely forgot about being gentle with Stephanie at first and just shoved himself in her all hot and heavy. When Stephanie tightened her hold on him, he realized what he had done.

"Oh fuck Stephanie, I forgot to start gently with you at first. I'm sorry. I was so turned on I forgot, baby."

Putting her hands on his cheek.

"Will you stop that? It needed to be done and I was right about it stinging, but now I'm fine. I don't want you to stop."

She wrapped her legs around his waist. He was still hard inside her and he slowly started to move back and forth.

Hunter wanted to make sure she came first. He lowered his hand and put two fingers inside her hot mount, along with his erection. He moved his fingers back and forth, changing the intensity while he kept pushing in and out of her. It didn't take long for him to hear...

"Oh my God... Hunter,... what are you... doing to me?"

At that moment, with his fingers speeding up their motions, and his body pumping into her harder and faster, she climaxed, with Hunter following right behind her. Both of their bodies were shining from love making and panting hard. They couldn't talk, much less move.

She finally was able to tell him.

"God Hunter, I had no idea it would feel that good."

He settling himself on his side next to her.

"Steph, you never thought of pleasuring yourself before now?"

"You have to realize, Hunt, that I really didn't have any girlfriends to hang out with and to talk to. I read about it in magazines, but really since I had no idea how it would feel, it didn't seem that big of a deal."

"But didn't you overhear other women talk about it?"

"No, not really. At school I would get bits and pieces from the girls, but I never really sat down and had a serious talk about it. My mother tried to talk to me about it, but I assured her that I had no interest in being with any guys and that I learned most of it at school, which I really didn't, but I didn't want my mom to bother. To be honest, at that time it just was not important to me. My focus was on school, not men, much less anything else."

Hunter simply stared at her.

"Wow."

It didn't take him long to get aroused again. He grabbed her by the waist and pulled her over on top of him.

Giving him her sexy smirk.

"Again?"

Hunter nodding his head.

Stephanie couldn't wait.

"Oh goodie."

The rest of the night was a constant do-over in pleasure seeking. Hunter was a magician when it came to condoms. He had them in his pants pocket, in both pockets of his jacket and there were still some condoms left on the nightstand.

***

Stephanie had surprised herself, since this was the first time she had been naked with a man. She knew she had done something right and guessed it must have been those romance novels that she read and definitely those two x-rated movies she had rented. Thank God she somehow subconsciously remembered.

"Damn, Steph, I want this to last all night. I have never been with anyone who has made me feel so alive and thank God you chose me. I don't want the night to end."

Their passion ignited yet again and he slowly put himself back into her. She looked at him and nodded. Letting him know that she was OK and to continue.

It felt so good to have him in her. Leaning over while putting her hands on each side of him, she slowly raised her hips up and down moved them in a slow circular motion.

"Your killing me, Steph. Sweetheart, we have all night. How about this time you get under me, because it's my turn to make you scream."

"Well, if you say so."

The night was magical for both of them. They couldn't get enough and the night was still young. They made love for two more hours, then went to the kitchen and ate, went back to bed and made love some more. After couple hours more of making love, with after sex talk they decided to take a shower, only to continue where they left off in the shower. Once they were out of the hot shower they cuddled into each other and finally fell asleep.

CHAPTER SEVENTEEN

It was eight in the morning, Hunter's iPhone started to ring like an alarm clock. He reached for the cell and turned it off. He turned back to look at Stephanie, making sure she was still asleep. The woman was out cold and no wonder, they had been pretty busy with each other three-fourths of the night. Before they decided it was time to sleep he had set his iPhone alarm clock so he could call his aunt to see if he was needed. He carefully got up without waking Stephanie and walked into the bathroom and closed the door.

"Hey, auntie, just wanted to check up on you guys since I didn't come home."

"Hi, baby! Your sister and I are doing great. As soon as Anne finished her breakfast she went directly to see Patches and has been there since. You know Hunter, it's really amazing to watch the two of them. Anne doesn't even need to use a rope when she walks the filly. All she has to do is start walking and the little filly just follows her. I am so proud of her, Hunter."

"I had a feeling they were going to click. They're going to be great buddies."

"Well, with that said, I don't want you planning on coming home today. You need this and if I say so myself, you need Stephanie. I don't think you could have found a more perfect person. I get good vibes about the woman. Please, Hunter, you need a break from us. We have been a little concerned for you, but the two of us are so excited now that we've met Stephanie. Hey, if Stephanie has no plans, why don't you stay with her for the weekend and we'll see you Sunday evening."

"I don't know what to say, Mil. You're right though, Stephanie has become special to me and it makes me happy that the both of you feel the same way. Thanks, auntie. I'll see if Stephanie has plans for the rest of the weekend."

"Good, then I hope to see you tomorrow night, OK? I love you, Hunter."

"OK, Mil, I love you too, thanks. See you tomorrow night."

No sooner had he hung up than he heard Stephanie yawn as she was stretching. He opened the door to see her sitting up all groggy-eyed. He bet she was still half asleep.

As she started to lie back down she patted the bed. He knew she was telling him to come back to bed. Which he was happy to oblige. Scooting back into bed, pulling her body back into him, Hunter could tell Stephanie had fallen back to sleep. He had to smile because he couldn't get over how easy and natural it felt to be with her.

Later they had breakfast. He was rinsing the dishes while Stephanie put them in the dishwasher, when the phone rang. Perfect timing. He looked to see who was calling and answered.

"Hey, Rob my man, what's up?"

"Paula and I are going to ride to our cabin in Columbia and wanted to know if you were game also. It will be an overnighter and we'll be back sometime Sunday evening. I already talked to Jake and he said he'll see us up there. Apparently he was indisposed for a while."

Hunter said with a chuckle.

"Indisposed huh. Well, what's her name?"

Typical Jake.

"Have no idea, but thought the same thing. Paula is going to call Stephanie once I get off this phone to see if she's game also."

"No need, I'm with her right at this moment."

For a minute Hunter thought Rob had hung up.

"You still there Rob?"

"You're shitt'n me, right? Since when did you two get together and why am I always the last one to find out? I bet Paula had an idea and never said anything to me."

All Hunter could do was laugh, for it was typical with Rob, being the last one to find out the latest news. Although, Hunter knew the man's world was limited to a small list. Rob's life comprise of his work and work crew, his 48 PanHead, his bartering for his toys and the love of his life, Paula. That pretty much was it. He was content with just that. Hunter could see why. Paula was a tough, little one, but inside that beautiful woman had a tender heart for all, unless you made her mad. Then all bets were off. She amazed him. She would give the shirt off her back, yet put you in place if need be. Not many women were like her. Except Hunter had a feeling Stephanie and Paula were similar. That's probably why the two women had hit it off so fast and easily.

"Well, Rob, this must be a first for you. You're the first to find out, since Stephanie and I just got together last night."

"Yeah, but I betcha Paula had an idea. She's like that you know."

"Yeah, no doubt."

"Well, Hunter, it's going to be a good time. I also talked to Spike and he won't be able to go. He's out of town visiting someone."

"And again I say, what's her name?"

Rob laughed.

"Well, since Steph is with you, let Paula talk to her. She's been poking me for the last minute to give her the phone."

A second later Hunter heard.

"Damn it, woman, hold on. Hunter is getting Stephanie right now."

Shaking his head and laughing he looked to see Stephanie watching him, trying to figure out who and what the hell he was talking about.

"Baby, Rob's on the line and says Paula wants to talk to you. She'll explain everything."

With that he handed her his cell phone.

"Hi Paula."

"Well, I'll be dipped in shit. I had a feeling about the two of you."

No sooner had Paula said that than Stephanie heard Rob yelling in the back ground.

"Ya could have told me!"

"Oh hush," was Paula's reply.

Stephanie couldn't help but to laugh.

"You two are so cute together."

"Yeah, we are and I love him to death, but quit changing the subject, which is about you and Hunter."

"What about me and Hunter?"

As she said that she looked at Hunter. He had the biggest grin on his face and that's when she realized that everyone was soon going to know what was going on between the two of them. Well, she knew it was bound to happen sometime, but damn this was fast.

"Oh, honey, it was obvious when I saw the sparks fly between you two. I'm sure I wasn't the only one to notice, with the exception of my sweet hubby."

Stephanie heard Rob yell.

"I heard that."

"Well, damn, Paula. It was that obvious?"

"Yeah, it was. Jake and I could see between the two of you, the fireworks were a blazin'. Even though the two of you were desperately trying to avoid each other as much as possible. But it was obvious, even when I would catch you both trying to be sly and not be caught."

"You've got to be kidding me. Even Jake figured it out before Hunter and I ever did? How is that even possible?"

"Well, to be honest, it was Jake's idea of moving the spark between you two even faster and he metaphorically decided to put a torch up Hunter's ass to get him moving."

"Paula, what the hell are you talking about; moving the spark and putting a torch up his ass?"

"OK, Jake will probably kill me, but what the hell.

Remember when we all rode to Cambria? Well, all I'm going to say is that Jake made it a point to make Hunter realize that if he didn't act soon enough he was going to lose out. And from what I can see now, it looks like Jake was right."

"You've got to be kidding! Oh my God. I feel like an idiot. Wait till I tell Hunter. He just might freak out."

Laughing, Paula finally got herself under control.

"I don't think that will happen. Because Hunter is smart enough to know if it wasn't for Jake's mingling, you guys would still be avoiding each other. So no, Hunter will not get upset. In the long run he will probably thank Jake."

"Oh my God," was all Stephanie could say.

Again Paula broke out laughing.

Hunter had not moved away and was listening to the one-sided conversation and kept repeating.

"What? Torch what? Up…ass…what?"

Stephanie finally put her finger up against his mouth to hold him off from more questions.

"Anyway, the reason that I wanted to talk to you was because some of us are going to Columbia to our cabin today and wanted to know if you're interested to ride with us. We would be leaving back for home Sunday evening. So do you want to go?"

"Well, I'm game, but let me talk to Hunter and see what he says."

"Well how about this? If you guys decide to ride don't bother to call, just meet us at our place in three hours, OK?"

"OK. I'm definitely game, but I'll leave it up to Hunter. Gotta go, hope to see you in three hours."

Stephanie hung up and just stared at Hunter. With a questionable look on his face, held his arms up with palms facing upward.

"What was that about?"

Stephanie explained.

"Jake and Paula had seen the attraction between the two of us from the beginning and Jake apparently had hoped we would finally get together on the Scenic One run."

Hunter looked up to the ceiling and just started to laugh.

"Well I'll be damn. That conniver."

"So you're not mad at him."

"No, what I should be really doing is thanking him."

"Well, that's exactly what Paula said you would say. Damn, these people sure do know you."

"Yeah, they do. Anyway, I'm game to go if you are."

"Perfect, I was hoping you wanted to go. It sounds like it's going to be fun. Paula says to make sure to be at their place in three hours."

"Then how about if I go to home and pack up and come back with my bike? Then we could leave for their house from here."

With that he gave her a passionate kiss and left. Stephanie was excited and started to pack light for her one-day trip.

***

The sky was blue, with a slight breeze that cooled them off as they rode. They had lucked out again with great weather. They arrived at Rob and Paula's Columbia place. The house had a beautiful white wraparound porch that surrounded the first level of the two-story house Rob and Paula calls the cabin. The four of them were sitting around the deck drinking brewskis when they heard a Harley approaching. Knowing who it was, they all got up and went to greet Jake. Jake was not alone on his bike.

Hunter knew that Jake's back warmer was the woman who had him indisposed earlier. It just made Hunter smile, for Jake was always quite the charmer and women always gravitated towards him. Jake usually was more attracted to brunettes, but Hunter noticed some of this woman's strands of hair were practically platinum blond. But when this woman took off her helmet her black braided hair fell down her back.

As Jake got off his bike, he raised his hand toward the group.

"Hello, my countrymen, I bring glad tidings."

"Oh, shut up and get over here, so we can meet you lady friend."

Was Rob's response.

Hunter couldn't help but laugh for he knew the fun times had just begun. Putting his arm around Stephanie, he saw Jake gave them a big smile. Hunter knew Jake was patting himself on the back and Hunter was going to make a point to thank Jake sometime during this trip.

Stephanie finally saw another side of Robert, besides being a hard worker and loving husband. The guy was just as crazy and quick with the smart-ass remarks as the rest of the them. She had witnessed his sense of humor at work, but now she was seeing more of that man and his craziness and it just cracked her up. She felt so good being around these people.

The next day they decided to enjoy the late morning and rode their bikes to the St. Charles Saloon in Columbia, a few miles away. Jake and his lady friend, Cindy, decided to ride up to Pinecrest Lake for a couple of hours.

Once the two women finished their drinks Paula wanted to show Stephanie the cute gold mining town of Columbia that was just down the street, walking distance from the bar. Paula's main goal was to eventually stop at Columbia's old brick candy store.

Even before she walked in the candy store, Stephanie's sense of smell took over as her nose took in all of the different types of delicious chocolates. Once she walked in she saw a large inverted U-shape oak glass counter with large round glass containers on top, filled with a variety of multicolored sugar candy like taffy, licorice, sugar canes, and lollipops.

Stephanie was impressed with the tiny town of Columbia. It felt like she had stepped back in time. The buildings, were kept exactly as they had during the Gold Rush. There was a post office, a carriage stop to purchase their tickets to ride the stage coach and small stores and restaurant. At one end of town was a small jail and at the other end was the blacksmith's works. What really pleased her was the old-fashioned brick building of the candy store.

The two women were sitting on the old wooded bench in the front of the candy store, enjoying their fudge, when three rough-looking guys came up to them, apparently wanting to start up a conversation.

"Hey, ladies, what are you two doing here all by your lonesome? You know you two shouldn't be here all by yourself without someone to watch out for you."

Paula looked at the three guys as if they were apparently slow.

Addressing the guy that was talking. "We…are…sitting…here…eating…our…fudge."

Mr. Big Stuff puffed up his chest.

"Well, maybe we should stay here for your protection."

Paula shook her head and smile at them knowing Mr. Big Stuff was learning impaired.

"What protection? You mean from the ferocious bushy-tailed squirrels that live in the trees? Sorry, we don't need or want your protection. Thanks all the same."

Mr. Big Stuff would not take the hint to leave them alone, while Twiddle Dee and Twiddle Dum just stood there grinning like a pair of idiots.

Mr. Big Stuff spoke up again.

"Sorry babe, but that's not going to happen. I think it would be better for the both of you just to come with us and we'll make sure you have a good time."

Stephanie could tell that Paula was getting ready to lose it. Paula took a deep breath to reply.

"You know, I bet when you took an IQ test your results were negative."

Stephanie had to hold back her laugh. She got up from the bench she was sharing with Paula and looked at her.

"Let's head back."

Paula joined Stephanie and started to walk but the three guys were standing in front of them were blocking their way out.

Now Mr. Big Stuff acted insulted.

"Who the fuck do you think you are? You two are not going anyway, except with us."

She was now getting pissed and moved in front of Paula,

looking directly in Mr. Big Stuff's face.

"You guys need to back off and let us pass by."

Twiddle Dee and Twiddle Dum moved aside, but Mr. Big Stuff grabbed Stephanie's arm and pulled her towards him.

"Hey bitch, you're not going any ..."

That was as far as he got. Stephanie slammed her heel on Big Stuff's booted foot. The idiot screamed and started to lean forward. She grabbed his shoulders and lifted her knee, connected to his balls. The guy's face turned beet red as he tumbled over. Stephanie movements were fast, it took seconds for the man to end up on the ground. His buddies moved even farther from the two women, as Twiddle Dee cupped his hands over his private area to cover his own balls.

After they passed the guys, Paula turned to Stephanie.

"Where in the hell did that come from? You are one surprise after the other, aren't you, woman?"

"Self-defense class, thank you very much, but I was hoping I wouldn't ever have to use it."

Once they finished laughing, they looked up at the same time to see Hunter leaning against the building, arms crossed against his chest, looking directly at Stephanie with his eyebrows lifted as high as they could go. While Rob, as he looked at his Paula, had his hands in his his back pockets and the biggest-ass grin on his face .

Stephanie was surprised.

"How long have you guys been standing there?"

Rob walked closer to his wife and pulled her to him.

"From the beginning of you're conversation with the guy."

Still surprised, Stephanie looked at Hunter.

"Well, what if one of those guys tried to do something?"

Hunter pulled away from the building,

"That wouldn't have happened. We would have done something about it, but it looked like you took care of the problem and fast."

He gave her a smile.

"I'm proud of you, woman. Anything else about you I need to know?"

He grabbed her and gave her a big hug, along with a short passionate kiss.

"You're amazing."

Hunter whispered in her ear.

Just then they heard a Harley coming towards them and again they all knew who that was. As soon as Jake pulled up to them with Cindy, he knew something was up.

"What did we miss?"

Rob was happy to repeat all that happened.

"Damn it, I missed the whole thing. Shit, next time I'm not leaving you guys. We missed out on all the fun."

Rob just shook his head.

"Let's go back to the cabin and barbecue some steaks."

"OK," Jake said. "We'll meet you there."

Then rode off again.

It didn't take the four of them long to get to their bikes and head for the cabin.

CHAPTER EIGHTEEN

The weekend was fun and they rode back together splitting up as they reached the turnoffs heading to each of their homes. Hunter followed Stephanie to her house. He needed to be with her for a little while longer and it was still early evening and he just wanted more of her.

They rode the bikes into the garage and she closed the garage door. She got off her bike.

"I thought you were going to head for your place."

Hunter gave Stephanie one of his sly yet sexy looks.

"I have a little while to kill before I should head for home and wanted to still be with you."

"Well, that would be great. Have any idea what we should do?"

She couldn't keep a straight face and started to laugh.

"Oh you are one fine tease aren't you?"

She bent down and grabbed her saddlebags.

"Yes, I am."

Hunter followed her as she entered the kitchen through the side door in the garage. His eyes were busy staring at that fine piece of ass. Damn, how did he get so lucky. This woman was incredible. As soon as she put her saddlebags on the kitchen table Hunter reached over and pulled her back against him.

"I have wanted you for the last twenty four hours."

She turned to face him.

"Well, at least we got to sleep together. Even though we

couldn't do anything about it, I got to be near you."

"And you will again, I promise."

He bent down and they started a passionate make-out session, acting like they weren't getting enough. Hunter picked her up and took her to her bed. The sensual love fest did last a couple of hours. Both of them were in heaven.

***

Hunter steered his bike into his garage and went straight to the barn to see how Patches was doing. He was not surprised to see Anne still with the little filly, talking away to her and feeding her some apple slices.

Hunter walked in Blaze's stall, next to Patches, giving his horse attention.

"Hi, Hunter. Did you have a fun getaway?"

"Yes, I did, thank you."

"Well, don't thank me, you needed it. Hey, when is Stephanie going to come over? I want to show her how I can walk Patches without using a rope. She just follows me all around. I sure love Patches, Hunter."

"I know you do, baby, and it sounds like Patches feels the same way about you. I'm proud of you, Anne."

"I don't want to be away from her. I know I have to go to school, do my homework, eat dinner and finish my chores, but otherwise I want to be with her."

"Yeah, but don't forget your friends."

"Oh, I know and I explained to them that I won't be able to do anything for awhile until Patches starts to get back to normal. But I also told them that they can come over and visit whenever they want."

"Well, that's good, at least you let them know. Have you eaten dinner yet?"

"Yeah, that's why I'm here now giving Patches some treats. She and Blaze looks forward to their treat around this time. She's also eating well. I've been giving her what's written down, and her appetite is getting so much better. I'm so proud of her. Oh, you need to see how Patches and Blaze communicate with each other. Make sure to listen them when you're brushing Blaze. It's cute."

"I definitely will do that and Patches will be back to normal in no time. I'm going to head on inside. What time did Auntie say for you to come in for the night?"

"Well, since I finished my weekend homework and cleaned the kitchen she said to come in around nine p.m." She looked at her watch. "Which is fifteen minutes from now."

"OK, sweetheart, I'll see you inside."

Hunter left the barn and walked toward the house. He felt good. Mil was right. He did need this time off.

"I heard you arrive" Aunt Milly said when he came into the kitchen. "I hope you guys had a great time in Columbia."

"Yeah, it was fun. As usual we did a lot of laughing."

"Hey, you know what? I've been thinking, why don't we have some kind of a holiday get-together and have the whole gang over? I'm sure Anne would love it and maybe we can have a nice game of poker. I can ask my poker gals also."

"Yeah, that sounds great. I'll bring it up to Jake. Since it's only September we'll have enough time for everyone to vote on which holiday to celebrate. The highest votes win."

Before Hunter could walk off, his aunt Mil put her hand on his arm, tenderly looking at him.

"I'm so glad you and Stephanie got together. You two look like you were meant for each other."

"I'm glad too. I agree there is something going on between the two of us and it feels good. You know, knowing how you and Anne feel about Steph makes it even better. That is important to me."

"Well, all I can say is you have good taste."

"Yeah, I definitely agree with you on that."

CHAPTER NINETEEN

Stephanie was busy on the PanHead computer, designing for the new order she had recently received, when Paula walked in and sat down in front of her, looking upset.

"Paula, what's wrong?"

"Spike's reason for not coming to Columbia with us is here, razzing Spike now. He gave me the 'go somewhere look,' so here I am."

"Who is she, Paula? What's going on?"

"About two months ago Spike and this woman became an item, but thank God not for long. You know how quiet and easy-going he can be. Well, I think this woman, Katie, was one of the back-ups for Linda Blair's role of the devil in *The Exorcist*. I'm not kidding, there is something really wrong with that woman."

At that moment they heard loud noises coming from the shop. Both women got up from their seats and ran into the work area, only to see some crazy broad throwing tools around the shop, thankfully missing the bikes on a stands being repaired, while Spike just kept working on the bike. When she saw Stephanie and Paula she stopped what she was doing, then looked angrily at Spike.

"Oh, now I see why you don't want to get back with me. That fucking cunt over there took you away from me!"

The crazy lady grabbed a huge heavy wrench. Lifting it up over her head with both hands, she moved straight toward the women. Stephanie took three steps closer to her, while Paula tried to hold Stephanie back to no avail. Stephanie grabbed the wrench with her left hand, then swung her right arm, hitting the crazed woman smack dab in the face, knocking her out.

That's when Jake and Hunter walked in and froze.

Jake knew he missed out again.

"What did I miss this time?"

Spike spoke up.

"If I were you I would call the cops and get them over here. Katie lost it and was going after Steph. By the way, Steph, good hit. Sorry you had to get involved. I had no idea she would come here."

Jake, being his curious self.

"Let me guess, you finally broke it off with the wacko? I'll make another guess, this woman is the wacko, since it looks like she colored hair again and it's about time. Damn it I missed the action again!"

Hunter hung up from calling 911.

"The cops are on their way."

He walked over to Stephanie who was still standing over the passed-out woman. He pulled her towards him and hugged her.

"Baby, are you OK?"

"I'm good. Paula and I heard a big ruckus in the shop and we just walked in here. The chick thought that I was Spike's new girl and went after me."

Spike, looking at Hunter and Stephanie, eyes squinted wearing a questionable expression as he looked back and forth between the two of them.

"When did this, (his finger kept pointing back and forth from Hunter to Stephanie) happen?"

Hunter ignored Spike.

"Looks to me like Stephanie can take care of herself."

Jake enthusiastically piped in.

"Spike, once the cops leave I'll tell you what happened this weekend in Columbia. Unfortunately, I missed out on that one also."

Paula went over and gave Stephanie a hug.

"You okay, woman? You gave me a scare."

"I'm good, Paula."

"Well good, because beginning Friday, you're going to start teaching me some of those self-defense moves. Too bad Rob wasn't here to see what happened. He's going to be pissed that he missed it."

Hands on hips Jake responded.

"Yeah well, he can get in line."

"Paula why don't we take a class together, you would learn a lot more than me teaching you and if would be more fun."

"OK that sounds great. Let's do that."

Hunter looked at Stephanie.

"Pretty soon the cops will be here and it'll be another couple of hours before they'll probably be done talking to you, Spike and maybe even Paula, but I would be surprised if you'll have to go to the station, but you never know. Anyway, if you don't have to go to the station, let's plan on going out eat lunch."

"OK. That's if my stomach has settled down by then."

The cops arrived within ten minutes of Hunter's call and the wild woman had started to wake up. As soon as she came to she stood up, glaring at Stephanie even though Hunter still had his arm around her. The wild woman started to rush toward Stephanie again, wanting to fight. Good thing a deputy was close enough to the wild woman to grab her before another incident happened.

The woman was going crazy screaming.

"You fucking bitch. Spike's mine. Stay away from him."

Hunter could tell the whole situation bothered Stephanie. When she turned around and walked back in her office, he followed her.

"You OK, babe?"

"Yeah, I'm fine. Even though the woman tried to hurt me, I still feel bad for her. Is that weird?"

"No, sweetheart, it's not weird. It seems you just have a tender heart for others. There's nothing wrong with that. As a matter of fact, it makes you a better person than most."

"Well, I don't know about that, but my heart goes out to those who are troubled. Something in their life was off and the result of it turns them into a negative. That's so sad."

"Maybe that woman will get some help because of the incident."

"I sure hope so."

One of the deputies walked in the office, saying he needed to talk to each of them separately. He started asking her questions. Hunter left her office and waited for the deputy to find him to ask more questions.

Stephanie refused to press charges, but asked if the woman could possibly get some medical and mental help. The deputy told Stephanie he would be transferring her to the hospital to make sure she didn't have a concussion, just to be safe and then she would be kept to talk to the psychiatrist on duty. Stephanie was glad this woman was going to get some kind of help. She thanked the deputy and he left to look for Hunter. She walked back to her desk and started working until Hunter came to get her.

***

The questioning was done and now Hunter and Stephanie were at a local cafe. Lunch was light for Stephanie. Her stomach might not have been upset as before, but she didn't want to chance it.

Hunter reached over and took Stephanie's hand and whispered in her ear.

"God, Steph, I want you now so bad. I want to go over to your place."

"Yes, definitely come over and –" Steph gave him a sexy smirk," – I want you also, right now."

That was all Hunter needed. He reached over and gave Stephanie a passionate kiss, then pulled back embarrassed.

"Sorry if I embarrassed you, but I couldn't help it, Steph. You drive me crazy."

All Stephanie did was laugh and placed her hand in his.

"Don't apologize, Hunter, because I want to be doing precisely what's on your mind. So let's say we're in agreement."

"My exact thoughts."

Hunter couldn't drive his truck fast enough to her house. Once Stephanie's front door was closed and locked, he picked her up, and rushed to her room, throwing her on the bed with him right behind.

He looked at his watch.

"We have about another half hour. Let's see what we can do to each other, what do you say?"

"Oh, you little devil, I'm all for a quickie, for now. It will last me until tonight. Will you stay over tonight, as long as you get up early to be with Anne in the morning before she goes to school?"

"I think I can manage that. I'll give Mil a call when I get back to the office to let her know. You know they were hoping that we would get together. They both like you."

"Well, I like both of them too. Now can we get back to business?"

"You don't have to ask me twice, woman."

The passionate kiss became a prelude to what was going to come. Hunter now understood how encompassing emotions could be when you found the right person. Stephanie was the person his heart had been waiting for.

CHAPTER TWENTY

Stephanie was full and sated. Sitting in front of the computer, she was unable to concentrate on her design. Her mind kept floating back to their less-than-half-hour quickie and man, she felt good. Hunter had the Midis touch and he knew exactly what to do with it.

In his office Hunter had just put down the phone from talking to his aunt when Rob walked in.

"I just heard what happened earlier today. I guess we don't have to worry about Steph not being able to take care of herself, huh? Jake's pissed because he missed out on the action. Again. Now I understand why he feels that way, because damn!"

"Man, Rob, I hope she doesn't get pissed off at me anytime soon. Jake and I had walked in when we see what's her name, Katie, falling unconscious on the floor. Putting two and two together we figured Steph punched her. And yeah, I'm also impressed, big time."

"Yeah, I agree and so does Paula. She says that she and Steph will be taking some self-defense classes together. She's all hyped about that."

"I think that's a great idea for Paula, since there will be times when you're not with her and this will build up her confidence when she is alone. Although that is not very often, but it would be good to know."

"Yeah, I so agree. I kept thinking about what if Paula had

been by herself when she was confronted by those three creeps in Columbia. You know it freaks me out. So having Stephanie around is going to be a big positive for our Paula."

"You know," Hunter said, "I've got to admit, she's going to be a big positive for me too, which is a shock."

"You're right about that. With you being so dedicated to your family, I have to admit I've never seen you interested in any other females since Paula and I started working here. So, well, I figured you would never hook up with anyone, but I'm damn glad you did. Just a quick FYI, you are different. By that I mean you seem even happier and you're not as serious as you used to be. Thank God. You know, my Paula had started getting concerned for you. She didn't think you should be without someone special. Besides Anne and your aunt and I kind of agree."

Rob cleared his throat. He needed cut the sensitive, girlie talk and get back to work.

"That's all I'm saying about that."

And proceeded to walk out.

Hunter just sat there dumbfounded.

"Well I'll be damned."

***

The next day Stephanie was putting something in the filing cabinet when Hunter quietly walked in her office. She felt someone's presence in the office and knew it probably was Hunter, but she didn't realized how close he was to her, until he leaned toward her ear.

"Thank you for last night. I'm going to be smiling all day long."

She turned to face him as she put her arms around his neck.

"Well, there's more where that came from. I, too, am very content. Thank you also."

Right then they heard Jake over the intercom calling everyone in meet in the shop. Grabbing Stephanie's hand, Hunter headed to where everyone was meeting.

When everyone was there Jake started talking.

"OK, everyone, since we're all present, Hunter wants me to

make an announcement. You and whoever, looking at Spike, (Mr. Ladies Man) are all invited to a holiday party at Hunter's place, but we have to vote on what holiday you want to celebrate and the date. Since some of you will be traveling to visit your family, the party will be a week before the holiday, or whatever you guys decide, so let's decide now. Any suggestions?"

Paula lifted her arm in the air.

"I'm game for around Christmas time."

Rob nodded in agreement.

The one who seldom speaks. Spike spoke.

"How about New Year's Eve? That way we avoid the two major holidays and we all will probably be home by New Year's."

Paula and Robert looked at each other and nodded enthusiastically. Rob spoke first.

"Yeah, we're game for that one also. We change our vote."

Jake looked at Stephanie. It was her turn for her input. He knew that whatever Steph wanted to do, Hunter would be game for it too.

"Sounds good to me. I also say New Years Eve."

"OK, then it's settled. A New Year's Eve party it is. I'll make sure to invite Jason and Sam also. And to make it easier on Aunt Milly let's make it a pot luck. For those who don't cook, bring your choice of booze and/or dessert. I will be bringing a keg of Budweiser and some fudge and maybe the fudge maker also."

That made the group laugh, because they all knew how Jake was with the women.

Jake continued.

"Milly and some of her friends will be there to play poker, so bring some ging, moolah, money, with you if you want to play. FYI, I hear those poker gals are pretty good, so beware."

Paula had been leaning toward Rob and talking quietly. Now she turned toward the group.

"We'll bring the tri-tip for all and we'll barbecue it. Even if it rains, Hunter has the BBQ blocked from the elements so it should be fine."

"That sounds great, but we don't all have to decide yet. Just think about it for now."

Jake clapped his hands together.

"OK, let's all get back to work."

They all broke apart, once that was said, going their own separate ways.

Hunter followed Stephanie into her office.

"God, Hunter, that is going to be so much fun. I can't wait. I'm trying to decide between two of my favorite meals to cook. Hey, maybe I should fix them for you first. Then you can let me know which one you liked the best. What do you think?"

"I'm game. When did you want to fix the first one?"

Stephanie had to laugh at his enthusiasm.

"Well, how about me fixing one of them for you, Anne and Aunt Milly?"

"I know they would love that and so would I. Aunt Milly mentioned that Anne has already asked when will you be coming over again, so how about Friday, so I can take you home afterward and stay with you the rest of the week-end. I already found out nothing is going on with the two females at home, so they wanted me to be gone."

Stephanie couldn't help but give Hunter the biggest grin.

"I think that is a perfect plan. Now go away so I can decide which one I'm going to fix and let me get back to work. I don't want the boss to think I'm slacking in my duties."

Hunter pulled her toward him, slowly lowering his head and gave her the most sizzling long ass-kiss, only to turn around and walk away with a smirk on his lips.

Silently Stephanie mouthed, "Wow."

That was all Stephanie was able to say. She reached for the desk to get herself grounded again. He sure knew how to throw her for a loop. For some reason it was then that she knew she was going to fix the Hearty Heros for them. Now she was ready to get back to work. How in the hell was she going to be able to concentrate when he kissed her like that?

***

For Hunter the day was going smoothly and productively until Jake rushed in. Hunter noticed Jake wasn't his usual easy-going self.

"Hey man, the sheriffs just called me since your phone and Stephanie's are both turned off. They said that Katie escaped."

"What the hell happened? How in the hell did she escape?"

"They said it happened at the sheriffs station. They had just brought her in when a fight broke out between two gang members. The deputy that was holding on to Katie ended up involved in holding back one of the gang members and that's when Katie simply walked out of the station."

"Ah damn, you know she's going to go after Stephanie, don't you?"

"That's exactly what the deputy thought might happen also. They wanted to make sure you guys watch your back until she is caught again."

"Thanks, Jake. I need to go talk to Steph. If she's unable to concentrate on her work, I'll just tell her to stop for the rest of the day since there's only three hours left of work."

"Good idea, but, Hunter, I don't think she should be alone until the wacko is caught."

"You're right. I'll talk to her about staying with her until this whole thing goes over, but first I need to call Aunt Milly. Thanks Jake for the heads up."

"OK man, see ya later and be careful."

Hunter dreaded having to tell Stephanie what happened. He didn't know how she would react. He knew he needed to talk to her now and headed to her office.

"Babe, sorry to bother you but we need to talk."

This was a first for Stephanie to see Hunter so serious. What the hell had happen?

"What's wrong?"

"Jake just told me that Spike's ex escaped."

That statement got her attention.

"How in the hell did that happen?"

Hunter proceeded to tell her all that Jake had told him. Stephanie turned pale.

"You know, sweetheart, under the circumstances I want to stay with you at your place until this whole Katie thing is settled. And before you ask I already talked to Aunt Milly about having Anne stay with her place and she agrees wholeheartedly."

"I'm just shocked she got away. Although that was quick thinking on her part. But do you really think she'll come after me?"

"I wouldn't put it past her, sweetheart. There is something definitely off about her and I'm afraid you're going to be her target."

"You'd better mention this thing to Spike so he can keep his eyes open too."

"I'm sure Jake has already warned him."

"Don't you think this woman would go after Spike first?"

"Yeah, she could, but she thinks you were the one who took Spike away from her."

"Oh. Damn."

"Yeah, so do you want to stop working and just go home?"

"No, Hunt, I'm fine. If I go home now I'll have nothing to do but think about her and I don't want to do that. But if I'm unable to concentrate I'll let you know. As for you staying over, I would love that."

Hunter shouldn't have been surprised at her reaction. This was one strong woman. He knew she could take care of herself, but the idea of her being by herself for now was not an option for him. He wanted to wrap a protective bubble around her.

"OK, sweetheart. I'm going to head for home and pack a bag to take to your place. I shouldn't be gone too long."

"OK, I'll see you when you get back."

Hunter walked to where Stephanie was sitting and bent down, giving her a passionate kiss.

"I'll be back."

He walked out of her office.

Stephanie just sat there staring into space. Once out of the zone she sat straight up in her chair, knowing where she was right now was safe. Katie wouldn't be able to get to her before someone saw her first. She knew once she got back to concentrating on her order, her thoughts would be only on that for awhile. Might as well be as productive as possible.

CHAPTER TWENTY-ONE

After work on Friday, Hunter followed Stephanie to her place to drop off her car and put together the food she was going to take over to fix her Hearty Heros. But before they headed out he was lusting for her again. He couldn't believe his unsatiated appetite for this woman. He just couldn't get enough of her and when he did, his satiation didn't last long enough. So now he wanted to make up for the time they'd been at work.

Stephanie walked in the living room carrying a bag with the food she was going to need. Hunter walked over to her, took the bag and put it on the living room table.

"Before we go let's have another, what did you call it, quickie? I didn't think working with you would be so hard. By that I mean, it's the hardest thing for me to do, without putting you on the desk and having my way with you."

She put her arms around his neck.

"Well, sweetie, we can't have that, can we?"

Stephanie rubbed her hips into Hunter seductively.

"Then we better do something about it, don't you think."

All she heard was a groan, then felt Hunter lift her up again, rushing toward her bedroom.

***

Their quickie was half an hour long, but they finally arrived at Hunter's house. As soon as Stephanie stepped out of Hunter's truck, Anne rushed over and gave her a big hug.

"You finally came. I have so much to tell you and show you how Patches is doing."

"I'm glad to see you again too, honey. How about if we do all that once dinner is over? That way we could go see Patches while you tell me what you have been up to with school."

"Oh good, let's go in. Auntie is probably finishing setting the table."

Anne looked at Hunter without saying hi and just smiled.

No sooner had they sat down then Anne started talking about the woman who escaped. Her face was a statement of concern.

"Stephanie, I know there is someone who might be mad at you and want to hurt you, but with Hunter there with you he'll protect you."

Stephanie knew Hunter wanted to tell his sister that she could protect herself very well, but there really was no need to. She was touched by Anne's concern. Before Hunter could say anything she reached under the table and squeezed his thigh.

"Thank you, Anne. I have no worries that he'll be there for me. I just don't want you to worry. Everything will work itself out and the woman will eventually get caught. It's really sad because the woman is troubled and needs help. I feel bad for her in a way."

"Well, I'll say some prayers for her that she gets help, OK?"

"That would be wonderful, sweetheart. Thank you, and I will do the same."

Hunter was really enjoying his hearty hero. He looked up from finishing what he was eating.

"Damn babe, those were good. What do you call them?"

"Hearty Heros. They are my fav. If I know I'm going to be home alone for the weekend with nothing to do, this is what I fix myself. I will eat it for every meal through out the whole weekend."

Milly added.

"I agree with Hunter. I've never had anything like this and it's so tasty."

Anne wiping her mouth, spoke.

"Me too, I loved em. Maybe if you write down the recipe, Hunter or Aunt Milly will fix them for me. And maybe someday you could teach me how to fix them?"

Stephanie was delighted.

"For sure, I would love too."

Aunt Milly was curious with what was in this delicious meal.

"Stephanie, I'm curious what are the ingredients in this hearty hero?"

Stephanie smiled.

"It's a pretty simple recipe. Let's see. There's the sour dough loaf, butter, ground beef, dry minced onions, chopped olives, catsup, mozzarella cheese and last but not least parmesan cheese. I'll e-mail this recipe to you, once Hunter gives me your address."

Anne clapped her hands.

"I can't wait to learn to make them."

Aunt Milly interrupted.

"Stephanie, why don't you and Anne go see Patches, while I clean up the kitchen."

Anne walked around the table and reached for Stephanie's hand pulling her toward the back door.

"Oh good, let's go, Stephanie."

Stephanie looked at Hunter wondering if he was coming too.

"I'm going to help Aunt Milly with the clean-up," he said, "so I'll see you both in the barn as soon as I'm done."

Stephanie nodded and walked out holding Anne's hand.

"Looks like you have it bad for that woman, don't you?" Aunt Mil said.

"Yeah, I do and it scares the hell out of me."

"Well, again I say, it's about damn time. A word of advice, face your fear, sweetheart. You can't go wrong."

"OK, OK, I got the hint, don't let this one go. You know, Auntie, I never thought I would find anyone as special as Steph and I was OK with that, but now I want more."

"Then just start listening to your heart instead of that damn fear."

Then Aunt Milly changed the subject.

"You know, the New Year's Eve get-together is going to be fun. Anne talked about asking three of her friends to come to the party and even stay over. What do you think?"

"If the loud noise from the party doesn't bother them, then I don't see why not. It would be good for Anne anyway, since she spends so much time with Patches now."

"For Christmas she has been hinting for a bracelet-making kit and a manicure and pedicure set. I think with those two things and two of her favorite DVDs to watch and we can't forget visiting Patches, they won't want to have anything to do with the grown-ups. She's going to have fun."

"Yeah, I agree. How about if we each get her one of the kits and one of the DVDs she likes. You know, I was thinking about getting her a dog, but with Patches taking up most of her time, I think I'd better hold off. What do you think?"

"I definitely agree. Give her another year."

"OK, I'll do that. And now that we're done with the dishes I'm going to head out to the barn."

"And I'm going to go back to my place to do some more writing. Oh and don't forget to give Steph my e-mail address, for her recipe.Those Hearty Heros were damn good. I think I'll take a couple of them home with me for later. But make sure you keep me in touch about that woman after Steph. OK?"

"I sure will, Auntie and I'll give her you e-mail address. Bye."

Hunter slowed down as he approached the barn door. He could hear Anne telling Stephanie about some boy in her class.

"He's really cute, but I don't know what to say when he comes up to talk to me, I get nervous."

***

Stephanie smiled as she remembered when she was Anne's age.

"I bet you he's just as nervous as you. And if he's in a class of yours, talk about your assignment, or about the teacher, or whatever went on in class, or even other incidents around school. Hey, how about asking him what his favorite sports are? Eventually you two will start to feel comfortable with each other. And let me tell you something, even as a grownup you still get nervous when you find someone you're interested in. That's how I was with your brother."

***

Anne was shocked that such a pretty woman could get nervous when it came to boys or men.

"Really! I never thought you'd be nervous about anything. You're so pretty, I bet a lot of guys liked you."

"Thank you, but I really don't know about the guy thing. My brothers scared all the boys away before I even found out who liked me. While I was growing up I was too busy with school and then my career to want to get involved with anyone until …"

Stephanie hesitated.

Anne replied.

"Hunter."

Stephanie looked down at her feet and smiled.

"Yeah, until Hunter. Don't tell him but when I first saw him, he took my breath away, he's so handsome."

"You really mean hot, don't you."

Stephanie couldn't help but laugh.

"Yeah you're right, I meant hot."

The two females were laughing when the subject of their discussion walked in, giving Stephanie a look that told her she was in for a long night of loving. Goose bumps crawled up her arms in anticipation.

Anne saw Hunter.

"Oh! Hi, Hunter. We were just talking about you, but I'm not going to tell you what it was about. That is between us two women."

Stephanie broke out and laughed again.

"That's right, it's between us two women. So don't even bother asking."

"OK, fine, I won't ask. But I am curious."

He pulled Stephanie next to him and positioned himself at

an angle so that Anne couldn't see him as he slowly rubbed that fine behind of hers.

***

Hunter needed to change the subject.

"What do you think of Patches, Steph? Anne has been doing a good job of taking care of her, don't you think?"

"Hunter, the horse looks so good. I can't believe how much weight that little filly has gained. Anne, you're doing a terrific job." Steph looked at Anne, "I'm really proud of you for showing how responsible you've been. Good job."

Anne blushed and smiled.

"Thank you."

Hunter looked down at his watch.

"How about you head to Auntie's house now. It's getting late and you need to get some sleep if you're going to the movies with Patty tomorrow."

"Yeah, you're right, I'm getting tired. Thank you, Steph, for making us dinner. It was really good. I want to learn how to make it."

"You're very welcome, the recipe is really easy to learn. I'll e-mail your aunt the recipe, OK?"

"Good, thank you."

Anne walked over to Stephanie and hugged her.

"Good night Steph, night Hunter."

"Night sweetheart. Have fun tomorrow and we'll see you Sunday evening, OK?"

Anne left them alone as she walked toward Aunt Milly's house.

"OK."

"How about if we head out to your place after I lock up the house? 'll get your purse for you."

"OK, I'll see you in the truck."

CHAPTER TWENTY-TWO

Stephanie had just closed the truck door when she heard the ringing of a cell phone. She realized Hunter had left his cell phone in the truck. She picked it up to read who was calling, then answered it.

"Hey, Jake, what's up?"

"Did I end up calling your cell by accident?"

Stephanie laughed.

"No, Hunter left his cell in his truck. I had just sat down in it. When you called we're heading back to my house . He'a locking up his place. Did you want to wait for him?"

"No, I'll just tell you what's going on and let you two decide. Spike and I are meeting Sam and Jason at Henfling's. I wanted to give you guys a heads-up in case you wanted to meet us there in an hour. So talk to Hunter. No need to call me back. If you decide to meet us, then we'll see you there and if not we'll see you two on Monday. OK?"

"Sure, Jake, I'll let Hunter know. Bye."

No sooner had she hung up then Hunter opened the door.

"Your phone was ringing and I saw it was Jake, so I hope you don't mind my answering it."

"Not a problem. What did he want?"

Stephanie relayed what Jake had said. The two of them decided they wanted to be alone for at least an hour, then head out to Henfling's, a small, well-known biker bar in Ben Lomond, the town that was next door to Boulder Creek.

Tonight they took Hunter's Harley with Stephanie leaning into his back. The small parking lot of Henfling's Bar was packed with Harleys, so they parked his bike across the street along with the six other Harleys already parked there. The place was jumping. Stephanie couldn't believe this small bar could hold all the people that were there, not to mention a band, which at that moment was jamming. What helped make the place fit all the people was the huge outdoor deck on the right side of bar and that was when they saw their group. Their four friends had taken over one of the large deck tables. Sam was the first to see Hunter and Stephanie. He stood up on the bench and whistled to them. Hunter raised his arm to acknowledge him, steering Stephanie towards them.

As soon as Steph and Hunter got close, Jason came over and gave Stephanie a hug, along with that mischievous smile of his.

"Hey, young lady, it's good to see you again. How's it been going at your new place of employment? Are they treating you good?

Stephanie returned the hug, while Hunter claimed her by putting his arms around her.

"It's good to see you, Jason. Thank you for asking. I love my job and the people over there. I'm really lucky."

She gave him another hug and went over to hug the rest of the group, leaving Hunter with Jason.

Jason gave Hunter a big grin.

"What the hell are you smiling about, Tinker Bell?"

"Well, Cupcake, I see Jake's idea worked, that's all. If I can put my two cents in, it's about fucking time."

It took Hunter a few seconds to say anything.

"What the hell are you talking about, Jake's idea? What was his idea?"

Jason lifted his hands in a surrender gesture.

"Oh no way, I'm not going to say any more. Go talk to Jake. Just want to say it's good seeing you and glad you came. Gotta go get me another drink."

Jason patted Hunter on the back and walked away.

Hunter greeted everyone and sat next to Stephanie.

This time Spike had some cute brunette on his lap, whispering sweet nothings in her ear, while Jake and Sam were busy talking to two women who just walked up to them and started flirting.

Hunter leaned into Stephanie and gave her a soft kiss on her cheek.

"Babe, do you want a drink?"

"No, no alcohol but a 7-Up sounds good. I also need to go to the ladies room."

"OK, let's go then. Be back, people, going to the bar."

***

No sooner had Stephanie walked out of the ladies room when she hears a loud female voice. The band had stopped playing, taking a break and was able to hear the woman.

"Hunter, is that you? How are you?"

She glanced towards the woman's voice. She spotted Jake and Spike with their two new women friends, walk to the bar. Apparently they, also had heard the high-pitched voice. Hunter was standing near the bar and watched the woman throwing herself at him. Stephanie didn't like what she was seeing but when she noticed Hunter's expression she started laughing, just like Jake and Spike were doing.

The closer she got to Hunter and the banshee, the more her bitch meter started to see red. Now was starting to get pissed. She couldn't believe she was jealous. She never had felt like this for anyone and she didn't like the feeling. But she also didn't like this woman with her arms around Hunter's neck like a vise. She had to admit that Hunter was trying to push her away, but the banshee wouldn't hear of it and kept throwing herself back at him. As soon as Stephanie got close enough for Hunter to notice, all he was able to do was go wide-eyed, giving Steph that *oh shit* look.

Stephanie had to calm herself before she did anything. She then tapped the crazy woman's shoulder. It was obvious that the woman was very high.

"Who the fuck are you? Can't you see I'm busy with this fine specimen of a man. Go away."

As the banshee turned toward Stephanie, she dropped her arms and Hunter backed away.

Calmly Stephanie replied.

"I am with that fine specimen of a man."

"Well, go away anyway, I'm talking to him."

The banshee reached for Hunter with no luck since he backed up.

But Stephanie thought otherwise.

"Oh yeah. Well, sweetheart, I really like your approach. Now let's see your departure."

She could hear Jake, Spike and Hunter laugh.

At that minute all could hear.

"Hey, Sandy, get over here and give me a hug!"

Banshee looked up when her name was called. She left Steph standing there as she ran to the other man. Hunter pulled Stephanie into a hug.

Jake and Spike walked toward them laughing.

Jake piped up.

"You know, that was a close call, Hunter. Great comeback, Steph."

Stephanie gave Jake a smile.

"You know the only time I react is out of self defense. So sorry, guys, to disappoint you."

"Well, it sure as hell came close. At least Spike and I got to see some action tonight."

Then Jake looked at Spike and the two women.

"Let's go and get our drinks. See you two at the table."

Then they walked off.

Hunter pulled Stephanie closer toward him.

"I haven't seen that woman since high school when we dated a couple of times."

Stephanie put her arms around him.

"I've got to tell you this is a first for me when it came to seeing red. I've never experienced jealousy before, but when I saw her with her arms around you trying to kiss you, I almost flipped."

"Baby, I'm sorry you had to see that. I didn't see her coming and had no idea she was going to act like that. Plus her being three sheets to the wind didn't help. But you know…"

Hunter started to rub her back up and down slowly.

"I kinda like that you got jealous. But I have to confess, that's how I felt when you teamed up with Jason when we went on our run to Cambria."

Stephanie's face turned puzzled.

"What do you mean teamed up?"

"When I saw him scoot his bike next to you and then ride beside you, it kind of pissed me off. So I didn't want to take the chance that he'd take over again at the restaurant so I decided to sit next to you."

"Hunter, I had no idea he was going to ride next to me. As a matter of fact, I was hoping you would but you stayed in the back. But I'm really glad you decide to sit next to me, because that's what I wanted too."

"Yeah, I know you had no idea, but that's when I realized you meant a little more to me than I thought. Remember, it had been a while since I was attracted to anyone. So being attracted to you threw me for a loop. But I'm a happy man now."

"I couldn't be happier, Hunter. Thank you."

They were making out like two teenagers, while the two of them could care less.

"Let's get our drinks."

He led her to the bar.

When they walked back out to the deck, Stephanie noticed that all heads looked up from the table when they saw them approaching.

Sam was the first to speak up.

"I hear Jason and I missed some action in the bar. Plus the other two incidents involving you, Steph?"

Stephanie's felt her face turn red.

"Don't look at me. I hadn't planned any of it. But I don't know why I attract stuff like that. Why do you think I started taking self-defense classes? It was getting out of hand."

Jason said as he laughed.

"You mean there had been more incidents then these last three?"

"Yeah, unfortunately, but I'm not going to talk about it now."

"You can tell me later, baby, alone."

***

Hunter gave her a soft kiss. Hunter was feeling brave at that moment and looked at Jake.

"Hey, man, what did Jason mean about your idea working?"

"Well, I was trying to be tactful when it came to Stephanie."

"Jake, you display the tact and sensitivity of a rampaging bull elephant. Now what did you do?"

Once everyone stopped laughing, Jake answered.

"Some of us at the shop could see the attraction between the two of you so I just mentioned something to Jason and well, he followed through with my suggestion."

That was when Stephanie started to laugh.

"You mean you had Jason pretend he was interested in me, while he made sure we were riding buddies."

With his sexy grin Jason looked at Stephanie.

"No, sweetheart, I wasn't pretending."

He gave Hunter a big ass smile.

"But I knew my limits when it came to you."

Hunter just growled, only to make the group burst out laughing.

Shaking his head Hunter said.

"OK, Jake, I got it, you don't have to go any further."

"Yeah, well good, because I've been concerned. It seems that for a while now you been 'off'. Never mind about running the company, my concern was you running a bath. You just weren't there, man."

The group roared along with Hunter. Good times were being had by all.

CHAPTER TWENTY-THREE

The group had been having a good time laughing and just hanging out with each other for the last couple of hours. Stephanie couldn't get over how once one woman left one of the single guys, another female would soon take her place. It was amazing to watch. These guys were like blocks of chocolate that women couldn't deny.

Stephanie leaned into Hunter's ear.

"Damn, Hunter, was it always like this with you guys when it came to the women?"

"Pretty much, babe, but don't include me in that anymore. I've got what I want now and I'm not letting you go."

"Wow, what a great comeback. To be honest, I have no right to be upset about what happened before I knew you, but thinking about the women who must have come on to you is scratching at my bitch meter."

"I know what you mean, because I wouldn't want to know any of your past guys either. But thank God you didn't have any that you were very interested in. So, babe, just know if I had met you before those flings, those flings would have never happened and will never happen again. You are the one I only want."

Stephanie melted.

"You make me feel good Hunter."

Hunter whispered in her ear.

"How about we head home so I could do more stuff to make

you feel good."

***

Stephanie's eyes lit up with anticipation.

"Let's go."

They said their goodbyes to the group and took off for home on his Harley.

Once Stephanie's garage door and the kitchen door were closed, Hunter grabbed Stephanie around the waist, pulling her to his chest, slowly and seductively using his body as he rubbed her.

"Baby, you have no idea how turned on I am when I'm with you. Even just thinking of you my body reacts."

As Hunter continued his seductive gyration Stephanie raised her right hand to the back of his neck and started rubbing back and forth.

"Hunter, that's exactly how I feel whenever I'm with you. I don't think I can ever get enough of you. I feel sooooo good with you."

"Well, let's go in the bedroom now so I can show you what you mean to me, because I want to ravish you right now."

"Then ravish your heart out. We'll eventually end up in the bedroom."

Hunter saw the green light and their clothes, boots and everything else they had on were off instantly. Being naked was all they could think of. Their love making started in the kitchen and continued in the hallway. Finally they fell on the bed.

They had no obligations for the rest of the weekend and they both knew what they were going to spend their time on.

***

Hunter woke up sated and happy as hell. His life was turning out completely the opposite of what he thought would happen. He must have done something right to be rewarded with Stephanie. He had been prepared to wait till Anne moved out. He never thought he would find someone he would be falling hard for, but fate had other plans for him. He was a lucky son-of-a-bitch to have his Stephanie. Every day he'd been inwardly saying thank you since he'd been with her.

He was waking up with the most beautiful woman he has ever met, his dream woman to be exact, with one of her arms wrapped around his thigh, inches from his dick. And at the moment he was starting to get hard again. He couldn't help but start to laugh, knowing this was so not like him. Stephanie started to stir awake.

Hunter softly rubbed her back.

"Morning, sunshine. How did you sleep, considering how little amount of sleep we've had?"

Stephanie arched her back as her taut body continued its morning ritual of stretching, exposing her nipples and her flat stomach.

She leaned into Hunter's chest.

"Mmmm, I feel really good. No complaints here."

Hunter lifted her chin as he bent his head to her. He had started giving her a passionate kiss when his iPhone rang.

Stephanie leaned over him to grab his phone.

"You'd better get that, it could be your girls."

She looked at the caller ID.

"Nope, it's Jake."

She handed him the phone.

He gave Stephanie a short kiss, saying thank you. Then answered the phone.

Hunter answered.

"Hey, Jake."

"I know it's the weekend, but would you mind coming over here for about a half hour and help me with my carburetor? I figure you're at Stephanie's and she is a hop, skip and jump from my place so you should be quickly back to your love fest."

Hunter gave Stephanie a concerned look, although she didn't know why.

"Sure, we'll be there. See you in twenty."

"Thanks, Hunt. Bye."

As soon as Hunter ended the call Stephanie asked.

"What was with that concerned look on your face?"

"Jake asked if I would help him with working on his carburetor, but I don't want to leave you alone. Would you mind coming with me to Jake's?"

"Ah, Hunter, don't make me feel bad. I don't think it will take you long to help Jake, so why don't you go without me? This way I will be able to take a shower without any interruptions from a certain person's wonderful hands."

"Babe, I really don't like the idea of you being alone with Katie roaming around. She could be looking for you."

"I know and I understand your concern, but I've been doing pretty well on my own. I've had other confrontations with women like Katie and they turned out OK, nothing too bad."

"You know, woman, someday you've got to tell me about *all* your confrontations and how they ended. I'm still not comfortable about leaving you."

Stephanie had just finished putting on her skimpy underwear and t-shirt.

"Please, Hunter, just go. I'll be fine. Besides the sooner you get back, the more time we have to play."

Hunter was turned on again and wanted to show her how much. He knew she was right with the sooner he get this done.

"OK, I'm going to jump in the shower, then I'll head out."

Stephanie headed toward the kitchen.

"I'll make you some coffee to take with you."

"Thanks, babe."

His shower didn't take long. Grabbing his coffee in one hand Stephanie with the other, he pulled her close to him, gave her loving kiss and said bye.

CHAPTER TWENTY-FOUR

Once Hunter closed the front door Stephanie grabbed her cup of hot cocoa. She sipped the steaming, luscious dark chocolate while she walked to the bathroom. She wasn't a coffee person, but she sure loved her hot cocoa in the mornings. She turned on the shower and had started to take off her t-shirt when she heard a knock at the door. Figuring Hunter had forgotten something, she put her t-shirt back on and walked to the door with a big smile on her face. Her smile dropped once she opened the door.

She recognized Katie right away. Shock was an understatement. She had to collect herself fast before Katie decided to go haywire.

"Katie, why are you doing this?"

"You know why, bitch. You took my man away from me and I'm not going to take it anymore."

Stephanie knew she had to calm Katie down before the situation exploded.

"Katie, Spike and I aren't a couple. I'm seeing someone else."

"You don't have to tell me. I know your plot. You guys are trying to fool me into thinking you're with some other guy so I'll just back off, but that's not going to happen. I've been following you for a couple of days since I escaped. I started following you from your work, to your home and even from Henflings."

Stephanie noticed Katie was holding something in her right hand behind her back.

Katie rabbled on.

"Don't think I didn't see my man there with you. You guys aren't fooling me."

Stephanie was shocked that even when Katie saw her with Hunter she still thought she was with Spike.

"Katie, I was with my guy, not Spike. Didn't you see Spike with other women there while he was sitting at the table?"

"Don't try to trick me. I know that was just a ploy in case I was around. The man is mine and not yours."

Katie was getting madder.

"You hear me, bitch!"

"Katie, I'm sorry you think that but... "

Katie raised her hand over her head and started to swing the small bat at Stephanie. Again Stephanie quickly grabbed Katie's arm, raised her other hand into a fist and punched Katie right in the face, knocking her out – again.

Stephanie hated having to do that. The poor woman needed help. Good thing she had noticed Katie hiding something behind her back.

A neighbor who was walking his dog rushed over to Stephanie.

"Stephanie, are you OK?"

Stephanie hadn't had time to be upset. The whole incident had happened in minutes.

"I'm fine, she didn't touch me. Greg, do you have your cell phone with you to call the cops for me? I don't want to leave her alone."

Greg called 911. Then Stephanie borrowed his cell to call Hunter.

***

When Hunter looked at the ID caller on his phone and didn't recognize the caller, he almost didn't answer, but something told him he should.

"Hello."

"Hunter, it's me. Come home now, there's been a incident."

Then Stephanie hung up.

Hunter was beside himself.

"Fuck! I gotta go. Something happened at Stephanie's."

Jake grabbed his car keys following Hunter.

"OK, I'll drive. Let's go."

They were out of there in less than a minute.

Stephanie was still on the porch in front of her door when Hunter saw her and rushed out of Jake's car, grabbing her as soon as he got close enough. Seconds later Hunter realized someone was unconscious on the porch and knew it was Katie.

Stephanie didn't give him time to ask questions. She told him she needed to put on some pants and rushed into the house. She was gone thirty seconds, if that, when she came back out wearing a pair of sweatpants.

At that moment two Sheriff's deputies' cars arrived.

Hunter quietly asked.

"Are you OK, sweetheart? Did she hurt you?"

"No, she didn't get a chance to touch me, thank God."

The two deputies had walked up to the porch when they noticed the unconscious body.

Deputy number one asked, "Who's the one that did this?"

"That would be me." Stephanie answered. "This is the lady who escaped when she was brought in to be booked. Some kind of ruckus happened at the station and she was able to leave without being noticed. Her name is Katie, I don't know her last name though."

The deputy bent down on his knees to look at Katie.

"Before she's conscious and while we're waiting for the ambulance, tell me what happened."

Stephanie explained in detail what had transpired, pointing to the small bat at laid a few feet from Katie.

While Stephanie was answering the questions, deputy number two walked over to where Katie lay and handcuffed her hands behind her back.

The ambulance arrived. Kneeling, the paramedic then tried to wake her up. It took longer then expected. With Katie still supine she finally woke up, but she had limited movement, except for her head and legs. It took a few seconds for her to recollect what had happened. She started twisting her head from side to side and moving her body in the same direction she was looking at. They could tell by all this gyration that she was looking for someone. Once she recognized Stephanie, who was standing a couple of feet away, she started going crazy. The paramedic and EMT tried to subdue her with no effect. Asking her if she would let them check her out. The woman wanted nothing to do with them.

Deputy number one rushed to help the two guys hold her down. For such a small woman she put up quite a struggle. She kept screaming at Stephanie, not taking her eyes off her. The deputy had enough of being kicked and tied up her legs together. Finally they picked her up by the arms and dragged her to one of the patrol cars, still screaming.

The second deputy walked over to the neighbor and started asking him questions.

***

Stephanie was torn. Yes, the woman had tried to hurt her and continued to want to hurt her, but the poor woman's mental state was so damaged there was no place in her heart to be angry. The woman needed as much help as possible.

She rushed over to the patrol car where deputy number one was now standing.

"Please, I don't want to press charges as long as she is sent to get some psychiatric help. She is in desperate need of it."

With the deputy agreeing, Stephanie watched the two patrol cars drive off with Katie in one of them still screaming.

CHAPTER TWENTY-FIVE

As soon as Stephanie left to talk to the deputy Jake walked up to Hunter.

"What in the fuck happened? I couldn't hear what Steph was telling the deputy with all the screaming going on."

"Apparently Katie knocked on the door and Stephanie thought I had forgotten something after I left to go to your place, so when she answered the door she was surprised to see it was Katie."

He repeated to Jake everything that he heard Stephanie tell the deputy.

Jake looked bothered, remembering calling her a wacko, but now there was more to Katie's state then being jealous.

"It's too bad about Katie. She definitely is in need of some help. I remember telling Spike when he started seeing her that there was something off about her. Why do you think Stephanie went to talk to the deputy again?"

Hunter was starting to get to know his Stephanie and he admired her soft heart, which was making him fall for her even more.

"I bet she's making sure Katie gets some psychiatric help. It wouldn't surprise me if she tells the deputy that she's not going to press charges on her again. That's what she wanted the first time Katie was taken away during that incident at the shop."

"I've never met anyone that's had so many close calls as

Stephanie. Damn."

Jake's comment got Hunter to chuckle.

"Steph says stuff like this has been pretty common for her. That's why she started taking self-defense classes."

"That's right. I remember her saying something about that at Henfling's and I was curious then."

"I'll eventually find out." Knowing he would probably tell Jake as long as Stephanie was OK with it.

Hunter saw Stephanie walking toward them and reached for her as soon as she got close enough.

"I know I already asked you once but I'm going to ask you again. Are you OK?"

All that was bothering Stephanie was Katie's state of mind.

"God, Hunter, I feel so bad for that poor woman. She needs help and right away."

"Ah, sweetheart, we'll make sure she is getting help if that will make you feel better."

"Thank you, Hunter. Yes, that would make me feel a lot better."

Stephanie saw her neighbor still standing on the sidewalk looking her way. She excused herself from Hunter and Jake and walked up to her neighbor. She stuck out her hand towards her elderly neighbor to shake, then gave him a hug while his mutt was jumping up and down to get her attention.

"Thank you, Greg, for being here and calling the sheriffs for me and for letting me use your cell phone."

"I know the deputies left, but I couldn't leave until I knew you were OK. The woman was certainly troubled, wasn't she?"

"Yes, she has some mental problems that I hope will get treated."

Stephanie finally bent down to give the love and attention to Zorro, the mutt. Since she had lived in her tiny place she'd gotten to know some of her neighbors and had even dog-sat for Greg and Linda's cute little mutt. She loved that little dog.

"Hi, you cute little thing. I've missed you too. Yes, yes, thank you for all this love."

Zorro was licking her to death. Stephanie kept lifting her face, trying to keep the lick off her face and ended up having her poor neck licked to death. Jake and Hunter stood there laughing. Zorro couldn't get enough of Stephanie. Hunter couldn't blame the mutt.

"OK, sweetheart, I think I need to set you down since you gave my neck a nice lick bath. Keep being a good boy."

As soon as Greg left Stephanie walked back to the two guys.

"Now that the commotion is all over, you can go back to what you were doing, because I'm in need of a long warm shower."

Stephanie kept wiping her neck.

She continued.

"And before you try to change your mind about not going back to Jake's, don't. I'm fine. Right now I need to be alone and think and maybe say some prayers for Katie. So go back to Jake's, OK?"

That was all that Hunter needed to hear. He felt good that she was doing well considering. She was one tough cookie. Another point in her favor.

"OK, sweetheart. Jake and I will head out now so you can wash all those kisses from you neck. That dog was going crazy. Although I don't blame him."

That got both Stephanie and Jake laughing. Hunter gave Stephanie a kiss, then the two guys left to go back to Jake's house.

CHAPTER TWENTY-SIX

Two weeks had passed. Work at the PanHead Custom Harley Shop and Motorcycle Repair was busier than ever. The orders for bikes and even for new tank designs kept coming in. With the increase of business Hunter and Jake thought it was time to proceed with the expansion of their shop. There was no doubt about who their architect would be. Their friend Sam Collins has proven himself a well-known and popular architect. To them there was no other.

Jake gave Sam a call and decided that they would meet at Hunter's place on Saturday morning and have a BBQ later that evening. Sam was going to work on some designs for the shop and bring what he had with him to Hunter's. Hunter wanted to make sure Steph was there also, hoping she would give her input on the design. In the meantime, Jake headed to the fourth floor of the Santa Cruz County Office Building, where the Planning Department was located. He needed to get the permit started. They figured it would take two maybe three years to get the shop built and running. This had been a dream for quite a few years and now it was coming to fruit.

***

The relationship between Hunter and Stephanie was even hotter and heavier. The two were pretty much inseparable. Even their friendship grew. Having similar likes and dislikes helped make the relationship flow more smoothly.

Anne was in heaven when it came to her two favorite

women. Whenever Aunt Milly had work to do when it came to her writing business, or even when she had to leave town, knowing that Anne had Stephanie to take care of her was a huge load off her mind, while Stephanie and Anne's love for each other grew even tighter.

Patches had gained weight and was turning into a beautiful young filly, always following Anne wherever she went. The bond between the two was unbreakable now.

***

Today was Friday. Hunter got off work at 3 p.m. to meet Anne as soon she got off the bus. It was time for Patches to get used to a saddle while Anne walked her. He needed to make sure that Anne knew what to do when she starts to ride Patches.

Anne jumped off the bus steps and ran toward Hunter.

"This is so cool that Patches is healthy enough now to start her next phase, huh, Hunter?"

"Patches has only you to thank for that, Anne. You've done an excellent job as her handler. You can see how Patches has responded to you."

They walk toward the barn.

Anne lifted her chin up in a proud gesture.

"Thanks, Hunter. I knew we were going to be close. To me it hasn't been a chore. I just love being with her."

"Yeah, sweetheart, we all could tell."

Once they entered the barn, Hunter had Anne lead Patches outside. Patches knew something was up. She was acting nervous, bopping her head up and down, neighing, and moving her body back and forth, side to side. But all it took to calm her down was for Anne to put her hand softly on the horse's forehead. She rubbed slowly while she whispered to her filly. The change was instantaneous. Hunter was pretty impressed with his kid sister. He had never seen a horse settle down so fast. Not even his own horse. Maybe she was gifted?

Hunter was not surprised once Patches calmed down. It didn't take long for Anne to put on the bridle. Patches got used to it while Anne walked Patches all around the yard. Anne was in no rush. She took her time taking Patches to the stream that cut across the back part of the property to let her drink.

While Anne and Patches were on their walk, Hunter went inside the house to get dinner ready. After work Stephanie was going to come over to join them for dinner and watch the movie called *SALT*, which Steph had highly recommended.

By the time Stephanie arrived dinner was done and waiting. The three of them had enjoyed Hunter's dinner and where ready to watch the movie.

Hunter was getting ready to put the DVD in the player.

"What's this movie about?"

Stephanie and Anne sat together on the couch.

"Angelina Jolie is a CIA agent. The CIA believe she is a double agent and they're after her. There's a lot of action and the storyline is good. I love kick-ass women and Jolie always plays a good one."

Hunter sat on the other side of Stephanie, wrapping his arm on her shoulder as he watched the movie.

It was ten p.m., the movie was over and Anne had fallen asleep with her head on Stephanie's lap. Hunter picked up Anne and took her to bed. Once he came back to the living room Hunter held his hand out to Stephanie.

"You were right about the movie. That was a good movie. How about we sit out on the porch since it's nice outside?"

"Good, that had crossed my mind also. I'm glad you brought it up."

They sat on one of those swinging chairs, wide enough for two.

"What are your plans for each of the holidays, Steph?"

"Well, this year at Christmas my parents are flying over here and it's my turn to have all of them over. As for Thanksgiving, my brother, Brad and I are going over to Ryan's house in Pleasanton. But I'm also glad you brought that up, because I talked to Brad and I told him that I met someone who is very special to me. He said it was about damn time that I gave a man a chance to get to know me, but he also said it's time to meet you, so he invited you, Anne and Aunt Milly over for

Thanksgiving."

Hunter was hyped that Stephanie had the same feelings for him as he did for her. God, he felt so good. He wanted to burst out with a wallop of a scream. He was that happy. Hunter cupped both sides of Stephanie's face.

"Just to make sure you know, you've become so special to me, Steph. I never thought it would happen to me and I don't ever want to lose you. My feelings for you have gotten stronger each day."

Stephanie took the initiative and pulled Hunter towards her. She leaned into him and slowly kissed his forehead. Then she kissed both of his cheeks and the tip of his nose. She paused for a couple of seconds and gave Hunter one of her seductive looks. She finally laid a big one on him. All Hunter could do was moan.

They slowly pulled apart from each other and Hunter took both her hands.

"Steph, you know I've been thinking, since I don't like being away from you, well, I was wondering what you would think about moving in with me. I had a long talk with Anne and Aunt Milly and they wholeheartedly agreed and Anne wants you to move in like yesterday.

Stephanie was so surprised she cupped both her hands over her mouth. This was the last thing she had expected.

"Oh, Hunter, I don't know what to say. I do miss you even though you only live a short way from me, so yes, I would love to move in with you and your family."

"God, Steph, you have made me so happy. Once I tell Anne she's going to go crazy. How about I help you start packing on Sunday?"

"That would be great, thank you. I'll need to call my landlord and give him a month's notice. God, now that I know that I'll be moving in with you, I've got butterflies in my stomach. Hunt, I'm so excited."

Hunter gave her a soft kiss.

"Me too, baby, me too."

CHAPTER TWENTY-SEVEN

It was a productive Saturday. Jake had dropped by and was blown away by how much weight Patches had gained. He commented to Anne what a beautiful horse Patches was and what a great job she had done for her filly. To Hunter's surprise and Anne's glee, Patches took to Jake like any female would have. The filly was smitten.

With a smirk on his face Hunter whispered in Stephanie's ear.

"I swear to God, that guy is like a bucket of honey. All females swarm to him like a bunch of bees. He's something else to watch."

"Yeah, I see what you mean. Even this little filly is ga-ga, over him. Even animals know goodness when they see it."

With Stephanie's help, the new design of the shop was finalized with all in agreement about it.

It was decided the new building would be located behind the original PanHead shop, while the old shop was to be used to train students taking the motorcycle shop course. This would be there place to learn.

***

The weeks had flown by, the shop was busy and the holidays were getting closer. Everyone was looking forward to the nice break. The following weekend would be the Thanksgiving holiday and Stephanie, Hunter, Aunt Milly and Anne would head to Pleasanton to Stephanie's brother's place.

Hunter was looking forward to meeting the two men who were a gigantic influence on her.

After Hunter told Anne that Stephanie would be moving in, it had taken Anne five minutes of displaying her excitement to finally settle down. No sooner had she settled down when she decided to make Stephanie a "Welcome Home" cake. Hunter had a feeling he would have to fight his sister for Stephanie's attention. Hunter knew this was what Anne has been needing. Even though Aunt Milly was an important influence for Anne, he knew Anne would shadow Stephanie whenever she was around like a younger sibling. It was hero-worship plain and simple for Anne when it came to Stephanie.

With the help of Aunt Milly and Anne they now had moved three-fourths of Steph's stuff from her place to Hunter's. He couldn't wait till they were done. The holiday would be a nice break for everyone. He was glad that he talked Stephanie into start moving in right away. Having her with him every night, he couldn't have been happier, not to mention waking up sated. But the first night with her in his bed was something he would always remember.

Hunter relayed Anne's message "to start sleeping at the house now," which helped to finally convince Stephanie to do just that. So the day after Hunter had asked her to move in, she spent her first night staying over with them.

Stephanie was touched by the cake Anne made for her. It didn't take long for them to eat dinner and enjoy the cake. Stephanie was happy to follow Anne to her room while Anne got ready for bed. The two of them sat on the bed while Anne played her favorite music and they talked about boys, girlfriends, clothes and school. Girly stuff personified. Just thinking about having to have to talk about those topics with Anne made Hunter shiver. Maybe that was why she never brought them up to him, thank God.

After Anne fell asleep Stephanie walked into the living room where Hunter was channel surfing. He felt like a damn teenager. He was anticipating their private time together tonight.

Steph sat next to him on the couch and Hunter reached for her hand.

"Did Anne finally fall asleep?"

"Yeah, I think she would have fallen asleep sooner, but I could tell she was so wound up, so we just sat there and talked pretty much about everything important to a ten-year-old. I think she would have stayed up all night if she could have."

"No kidding. Now that you're here, Anne is turning this whole situation to her advantage. She's eating up the attention you've given her. You've become a blessing in disguise for our Anne. Thank you."

"Well, to be honest, I've always wanted a little sister and you couldn't ask for a better one than Anne. She's an amazing young girl. She's not showing any signs, yet of the rebellious stage some kids go through. Although I never did with my brothers always being around. You know, I feel sorry for you when she's at the dating age."

"Yeah, well, don't remind me. I'll probably be just like your brothers were with your male friends. Not a picture I care to see for another multiple years, at least."

Stephanie couldn't stop laughing, knowing Anne was going to put him through the wringer of worry.

"I'm sorry for laughing, Hunter, but I can just picture you when she starts dating."

"Yeah, well, like I said before, don't remind me."

That response made Stephanie laugh even more.

Once the two of them stopped laughing, Hunter started to rub her back slowly and seductively. Steph's whole body turned into one big shiver.

"Are you cold, sweetheart?"

"No, I'm not shivering because I'm cold. I'm shivering because of you. I remember when I practically ran into you the first time we met. And I swear to God, I had never before felt that zap of energy that went through me."

She looked into into his gorgeous green eyes, which were already eating her up.

"You touch me and my body automatically reacts."

Giving Stephanie his sexy smirk.

"You've got to realize, baby, that at that same moment, I felt the same exact energy and it threw me for a loop. That was a first for me too and I still love it."

He cupped her face and lowered his lips into a long, slow, seductive kiss, which only to turned into a wild, out-of-control seduction. The two of them couldn't get enough of each other. Their hands were all over each other. Then one of them instigated the removal of clothes.

CHAPTER TWENTY-EIGHT

They both realized at the same time that they needed to take this passion out of the living room. Hunter scooped Stephanie up in his arms headed to their room. Stephanie quickly grabbed the t-shirt she had stripped from him seconds ago.

He carried Stephanie down the hall. Hunter knew the noise factor between Anne's room and theirs would be minimal. For one thing, Anne always slept like a log and for another, his bed was located at the far end of his large rectangular room.

Stephanie, while in his arms, leaned back to face him as she wrapped her legs around his waist. And the make-out session started up again. They were so into their kissing as he pushed her against the hallway wall. Already shirtless, Hunter pulled off Stephanie's t-shirt, and the sports bra she was wearing, not letting them drop until they were in their room. He and Stephanie landed on his king size bed. Stephanie was in heaven with a man she never thought she would have a chance with.

Hunter grabbed for the top of her low-cut jeans pulling them off slowly, as his eyes devoured her body.

"God Steph, I can't get enough of looking at you. You are so damn beautiful." With a smirk on that sexy mouth of his he said, "And *hot*".

"And FYI, Hunt, you're not too bad on these eyes, much less anyone else's."

She pulled his jeans off and saw he was commando. She

didn't have to worry about taking off his socks because he was already barefoot.

"This is what I have wanted to do to you when I first saw that fine behind of yours."

She rubbed that fine butt, she always love to look at it and with her other hand cupped his beautiful jewels of his. Hunter, without realizing let out a moan.

"Damn, baby, you keep doing that, I'm not going to be able to last very long."

She gave Hunter one of her seductive smiles.

"Doesn't matter to me, since we're going to be doing this pretty much most of the night."

She squeezed his hard length, then loosened her hold. After a few more squeezes Hunter lost it. He couldn't control himself anymore and came.

With his forehead on her chest, it took him a few minutes to catch his breath since he was breathing so hard.

"Damn, woman, I have no control when it comes to you. I reacted like a damn teenager. All you had to do was touch me and I lost it.

"Which wasn't a first for me, by the way, when it comes to you."

He pulled off from her and walked into the bathroom. He came out carrying a washcloth and something else. Stephanie couldn't figure out what it was until he put the items on the nightstand. She raised herself on her elbows to watch him, but now that she'd figured out what he was carrying, she fell back onto the mattress and laughed.

"I can see you definitely plan on a long night of fun."

Hunter had grabbed a handful of condom packets and mind you, he had big hands, so there had to be close to fifteen on the nightstand. He sat on the bed and gently rubbed the warm wash towel over Steph's upper body, wiping off what was left of his release.

Stephanie remembered what she had been meaning to tell Hunter the first time they were together.

"Just to let you know, I was just recently checked and I'm

clean of any diseases, even though I'm now on the pill, so I'm glad you bought some more of those. You know, from the first time I was with you till now I meant to tell you, but you are so distracting."

"And just to let you know young lady, before you, it had been a while since I've had to buy those things. I had a physical last year and they also tested me and I too am clean. And since I haven't been with anyone for over a year, I figured I'm still clean. But how come you're on the pill since I was your first?"

"I've had bad menstrual cycles. With the doctor putting me on the pill to help and it has worked."

Hunter slowly crawled back on top of Stephanie.

"It's my turn to make you lose it and I promise you will lose it all...night...long."

"God, Hunter, you are one sexy son of a bitch. ...Pardon my vulgarity."

Hunter just laughed.

"Have I mentioned to you that your sense of humor comes out at the oddest times. I love it. You are not going to have any trouble keeping up with the rest of the smart-asses around here."

"Yeah and I'm going to enjoy every minute of it. I love to laugh. It just feels so good."

"Well, right now I'm going to show you something else that feels good."

He started to rub her thigh, working down to the calf. Then he slowly moved off her, while still between her legs and continued to caress her hip. He spread out his hand over her flat stomach, as he softly moved to one of her breast and teased the nipple. The taut nipple instantly reacted to his touch, and Stephanie quietly moaned to herself. She arched her back as soon as Hunter's mouth started to licked, sucked then nipped on the sensitive tip. She had no idea, while she was a virgin, that it would feel this wonderful , but now she was greedy for more.

The lovemaking lasted for another couple of hours. They

took a break, talking and then they fell asleep in each others arms.

Waking up to Anne screaming was not something Hunter expected and it scared the shit out of him. He and Stephanie jumped up from bed. Hunter slid his jeans on while Stephanie slipped on Hunter's t-shirt. Hunter was first to get to the door.

They ran in Anne's room to see Anne softly crying into the pillow.

Hunter rushed to the closest side of the bed while Stephanie went around to the other side.

Seeing Anne crying was not a common occurrence and he felt horrible.

"Sweetheart, what happened?"

Stephanie was kneeling down next to the bed and brushed the hair from Anne's face, not saying anything. She needed to let Hunter console her first.

"Hunter, I had a horrible dream about Patches. It felt so real."

"Baby, tell me what you dreamt."

Anne turned over on her back and realized Stephanie was there. She immediately grabbed for Stephanie's hand. With tears stills gliding down her face.

"It was horrible Hunter. Someone came and took Patches away and I was trying to stop him, but I couldn't. Will you go check on Patches for me? If she saw me crying I think she would get upset and know something was wrong."

"Sure, honey, I'll go check now. Stephanie will stay here with you, OK?"

"Yes, thank you, Hunter."

Once Hunter walked out of the room Stephanie rubbed Anne's arm up and down.

"Anne, do you have this type of dream very often?"

Anne was feeling better now that Hunter had gone to check on Patches and Stephanie was there with her.

"No. This is a first, but Aunt Milly told me how my mom's intuition was sharp at times. But she also said it was era..a... tic, something like that, they would happen once in a while."

"You mean erratic? And do you remember any of the stories about her intuition your aunt told you?"

"Yeah, that's the word. I remember she told me a story right before my mom died. Hunter was a teenager and he wanted to go to the movies with some friends of his, but my mom felt uneasy about it. She explained to Hunter she had a bad feeling something was going to happen. So she asked him if he would take the bus instead of having his friend pick him up."

"What was Hunter's reaction when she ask him to do that?"

"Well, my auntie said that Hunter had seen the few times Mom has had these weird feelings and dreams and it never failed that she was right. So he was glad he still was able to go to the movie and just met the guys there."

"What happened then?"

"After the movies some of the guys wanted to go ride around town, but Hunter told them he was needed at home and couldn't go. The guys ended up getting rammed into by a drunk driver. One of them broke an arm and leg. Another guy was in a coma for a week, but he recovered and was fine."

"Wow, that's incredible. Has Hunter ever talked to you about your mom's ability?"

"Yeah, he has. He said he always listened to his mom when she would get those feelings, but that was awhile ago."

They heard the back door slam. Anne sat up, anxiously waiting.

As soon as Hunter walked in he noticed the two anxious looks.

"Patches is there and is doing fine. She was surprised to see me so early and started neighing. So I gave her some attention for a little while, that's what took me so long to get back."

"Thank goodness." Anne said. "What a horrible dream, Hunter. I hope I never have that dream again."

Hunter loved his little sister.

"Do you think you can go back to sleep since it's only four am?"

"I'm still a little tired and having you guys here has helped. So yeah, I think I can go back to sleep."

"Good, we'll see you after we wake up too. Sweet dreams this time."

"OK. Night."

Stephanie bent down and kissed Anne's forehead.

As soon as they walked back into their room Stephanie had to ask.

"Anne told me about your mom's intuition and dreams. She said that whenever she got them she was pretty accurate."

"That's right. That's why I never questioned it when she had dreamt something. I don't think my dad ever got used to it. Those feelings gave him the creeps. I thought it was pretty cool."

"Has anything like that happened to you?"

"A couple of times, but nothing like my mother. But keep in mind she didn't have them that often either. And this would be a first for Anne if anything about her dream happened."

"Wow, that's incredible. What a gift. Although to be honest I hope this one dream of Anne's doesn't happen."

"I have to agree with you. You know we've had about an hour and a half sleep. Let's get some more sleep. We don't want to be dragging tomorrow since it's our day off."

The two of them got back in bed. Hunter cupped Stephanie, wrapping his arm around her waist. It took only a few minutes for both of them to relax and fall back to sleep.

CHAPTER TWENTY-NINE

Hunter's automatic alarm clock in his head woke him up early enough to quietly get out of bed and shower. He was in the kitchen, making one of Anne's favorite breakfast. Hash browns, bacon and eggs, for the three of them when Anne walked in the kitchen, ready to go and be with Patches.

"Morning, Hunter. Breakfast smells good. Is Stephanie still asleep?"

"Yeah, I'm going to let her sleep since it's her day off. But just in case she wakes up her breakfast will be made and in the oven for her. How are you feeling?"

Hunter grabbed Anne's plate and put food on it, then handed her the warm meal.

"Thanks, Hunt. I'm feeling good since I was able to go back to sleep."

"Did you enjoy your visit with Stephanie last night?"

"We talked so much about everything." Anne leaned over towards Hunter and whispered. "Did you know she never had a boyfriend in school? That really surprised me. I think she's beautiful and I really love her."

"To answer your question, yes, she told me about that and I agree with you. I think she is gorgeous too."

Again with the whisper.

"But do you love her also?"

That question took Hunter aback.

"You know, sweetheart, I never really thought about it. I was just so happy that she agreed to move in with us. Yet I knew she was special to me, so yeah, I think I could be growing to love her. Just don't say anything yet to her. I don't want to scare her off, OK?"

"Oh, I promise, I don't want to lose her either. It will be between you and me."

"With it being the weekend, what are your plans with Patches today?"

"We're going to walk to the creek again. She loves drinking from the creek. Hey, Hunter, when do you think I can start riding her?"

"How about we have the vet come and check Patches out next week and let him decide. But I wouldn't worry. I think Patches is going to get a clean bill of health."

Not even five minutes later Anne finished her breakfast. She was a fast eater like her brother.

"Oh good, I can't wait. I'm done eating so I'm going to see Patches now, OK?"

"Sure, baby, I'll see you later."

***

Even though Stephanie woke up a little sore, she felt wonderful. She knew who was responsible for it all and realized he wasn't in bed. She looked at the clock, 9:30 a.m. Their love session had lasted to early that morning. Then she remembered Anne having the nightmare. She figured she'd had about four hours sleep and since Hunter was already up he'd had less.

She got up and rushed to take a shower. Finally she walked into the kitchen, but unfortunately the kitchen was empty. She noticed a note leaning against the salt and pepper shakers

Anne and I are in the barn. Breakfast is in the oven. See you after you eat. Love

The note made her smile. She was not used to having someone take care of her besides her parents. It felt good. She didn't realize how hungry she was and enjoyed the breakfast Hunter had made for her. Once she cleaned up after herself, she rushed out to the barn.

As she stepped in the barn, the sight before her eyes made her stop in her tracks and her juices down below started to stir, again.

There was Hunter shoveling the hay into one of the stalls. The man was shirtless and was too beautiful for words. His smooth, muscular, tanned back had a slight glow from the sweat. His broad shoulders tapered down to his narrow, yummy hips. But what really took her breath away was when he turned around and she started visually feasting on his chiseled six-pack torso. Stephanie told herself to make sure she took a picture of him shirtless someday and to keep that picture close to her at all times. She would have loved to walk up behind him and rub herself all over him, to continue what they had started last night. But with Anne there she knew that couldn't happen.

"Good morning, you two."

In unison Hunter and Anne looked toward Stephanie, both with wide smiles. Anne rushed to her and gave her a hug.

"Hunter wanted to let you sleep in. Did you sleep good, Steph?"

"I slept great, thank you. How did you sleep?"

"Once I went back to sleep I didn't have any dreams and woke up feeling good."

"That's wonderful. What will you be up to with Patches today?"

"We just got back from a long walk. Now I'm just brushing her coat."

It seemed like Patches knew they were talking about her. She turned her head and looked at Stephanie and neighed.

Hunter came up behind her and wrapped his arms around her waist.

"It seems Patches recognizes you.

"You think so? Because she heard me the last time I was in hear and she didn't react."

"Yeah, but you have to remember she was pretty weak to react to anyone except Anne."

Anne gave them a big proud smile.

Stephanie nodded in agreement.

"That's right. I forgot how weak she was. Good observation, Hunt."

Patches keep neighing and bobbing her head.

Hunter kissed Stephanie's neck.

"She probably wants some love from you."

He lowered his mouth to her ear, for her ears only.

"Like I do. Just to let you know I can't stop thinking about last night."

He kissed her ear.

CHAPTER THIRTY

"Come, Stephanie, Patches is waiting for you."

Anne said eagerly.

Before she let go of Hunter, Stephanie leaned into him and whispered.

"Me too, my love, me too."

She lightly kissed him on the lips and walked toward the horse. As Stephanie got closer, Patches, started to neigh.

"She likes you, Steph." Anne said. "Hunter is right, Patches does remember you."

Stephanie kept her voice calm and low. She rubbed all along the horse's neck. Patches ate the attention up as she bent her head against Stephanie.

Leaning against the barn door, looking all his fine self, Hunter remarked.

"Yep, she remembers you."

Stephanie turned her head to look at Anne.

"I can't believe how good Patches looks. You've done a wonderful job taking care of her."

"She's a strong horse, Stephanie. Doesn't she look beautiful?"

"Yeah, she's a beauty. I can't believe how much she has filled out. She's gorgeous."

"Yeah, we think so too, huh, Hunter?"

"Your are right about that. You know, sweetheart, Stephanie needs to finish unpacking the last of her boxes so we'll be in the house, OK?"

"OK, Hunter, I'll see you guys later."

Anne turned back toward Patches and continued to brush the horses coat.

Hunter held out his hand to Stephanie. As she grabbed it he lowered his head and kissed her forehead.

"Let's go."

Once in the house they went into the office, where some her unopened boxes were stored.

"You know, Steph, being around you and not being able to have my way with you whenever I want is going to be the hardest thing for me."

"I know, because I thought the same thing back in the barn. I swear to God, Hunter, when I walked in, this heart of mind went pitter-patter as I watched that fine self of yours."

Giving Hunter a seductive look. "You made my mouth-water, ...my bed-spread, ...and my eye-ball."

"I made you do what?"

"And not to mention my cork screw."

She raised her eyebrows up and down fast.

Hunter broke out laughing.

"I've never heard that before, woman."

"There's more of them, but not going say them now. I need to take this box to our room."

Steph put her hand on a box that had Bedroom written on it.

Hunter picked up the box before Stephanie had the chance and led her to their room.

"God, I wish I could throw you on the bed and really show you what 'morning after' really means. It's going to be a test on our self-control to the max."

"Yeah, well, can you imagine if there were other little ones running around? Now that would be hard."

Steph couldn't believe what she'd just said. It came out without thought.

He walked closer to her.

"Speaking of hard."

He took her hand and put it right on the erection that gave her pleasure all night long."

She couldn't stop herself and cupped him as she squeezed him.

"God, woman, if you keep doing that I'm going to turn into a damn teenager again and shoot in these pants."

That 's when they heard the back door slam. They quickly parted and started working on the box.

Anne walked in their room.

"I've brought the mail in. There's even some mail for you, Steph."

"Wow, already. Boy, the post office doesn't fool around. I just gave them my new address just yesterday. And if I remember correctly we forgot to get the mail yesterday."

Hunter nodded his head.

"Right you are. We were all so preoccupied yesterday that we forgot. Thanks, Anne, for bringing it in."

Looking through the mail Anne lifted up a Netflix envelope. She knew what the movie was going to be. She had heard a lot about it Anne was excited.

"Can we watch this tonight? I hear it is really cute."

"What's the movie?" Hunter asked.

"It's called How To Train Your Dragon. I've been wanting to watch it."

Stephanie looked at Hunter.

"I'm not sure if it's your type of movie."

"That's OK Stephanie" Anne added. "If Hunter doesn't like it he'll go do something else around the house. Oh, I loved that movie. Count me in to watch it again."

"Yep, she's got that right." Hunter added as Anne handed the rest of the mail to him.

Then she walked out. They heard the back door slam as Anne headed back to her Patches.

Hunter reached in the big square box and pulled out some framed pictures.

"I've haven't seen these. I thought I saw all of them before you started packing. I love this photo of you and your brothers. How old were you here?"

Hunter showed her the picture he was talking about.

"Oh, that was behind all the other ones in the living room and had fallen back, that's why you didn't see it. I think I was eighteen. My brothers and I had just finished riding our dirt bikes at our parent's place in Colorado during Christmas holiday. It was so much fun."

"It's good to know that you also have a close-knit family. You have some wonderful memories."

"I know, I'm very lucky. But I our life has had its ups and downs too. There's no such thing as a perfect family, but we are very close to it. I think a lot of it had to do with the fact that there was always a lot of laughter in our lives. Laughter feels good and I believe it can be healing also. Laughter puts you in a positive state of mind."

"I totally agree. I remember my parents made it a point to do something fun. It was always enjoyable to be around them."

"You must really miss them. I can't imagine what you went through. You grew up even faster then you should have, but look at the wonderful job you have done with raising Anne. Your parents are very proud of you, Hunter."

"You're right, I miss them still, but they're together and watching over all of us. And Aunt Milly was a god-send for Anne and me. It has worked out real nice for the three of us."

Hunter took the picture from Stephanie's hand and placed it back in the box, then gently pulled her closer to him. The make-out session began. Again.

CHAPTER THIRTY-ONE

The Thanksgiving get-together was finally here. Stephanie loved where Ryan lived. The old part of Pleasanton was the part she loved and it still had its quaintly quality. Some of the older homes were still there. The street was beautifully lined with a variety of trees, some leaning into the street, while other tree limbs reach out onto the street, shading the area from Pleasanton's heat. Ryan purchased his house right after he started working for the California Highway Patrol (CHP), about eleven years ago.

Out of the three of them, Ryan was the most serious. Typical big brother, but a lot of fun. Same with Brad. But there was nothing serious about him.

Stephanie knew her brothers were going to like Hunter, but what really surprised her was how taken her two brothers with Anne. It reminded her of when she was growing up with them.

The two guys were somehow always paying attention to Anne and Stephanie could see Anne loved all the attention she was getting. But what left her really puzzled was watching her oldest brother, Ryan. If she didn't know any better she would have sworn that whenever he talked to Milly, which was often, his eyes sparkled with interest. This was a first.

He was reacting to her completely different from the way she had witnessed her good-looking brother reacting to other women. Ryan's relationships always ended up short but sweet.

Growing up with those two brothers of hers, she remembered how each of them had his own distinct way of finding women. She couldn't get over how those women went along with their temporary arrangement. But now call her crazy, for she had never seen Ryan react to any woman the way he was to Milly. If she didn't know better, her Ryan was growing more and more interested in this woman.

She knew Hunter's father was very young when Hunter was born. There's a ten year difference between Milly and Hunter.

Stephanie loved the idea her brother, at 39 years of age was falling for a wonderful woman.

Stephanie wasn't sure about Milly's reaction to Ryan, since she hasn't known Milly long enough to gauge any kind of emotion toward her brother. From watching those two together she could see that Milly was definitely enjoying herself, but if there was any kind of spark for Ryan, Milly was sure good at concealing it.

It really didn't surprise Stephanie that Ryan would be attracted to Milly, because she was one striking woman. A couple of times in the last few weeks, she and Milly had gone grocery shopping together and she noticed how men's eyes were drawn to her.

Milly had the most striking eyes. Where Hunter's eyes were green, Milly's eyes were a lighter shade of green you couldn't help but stare. Her shiny dark hair was the same as Hunter, but her hair was even shorter. She had the cutest pixie style cut that fit her oval face, bringing out her eyes.

It was fun spending time with Milly. Stephanie even went to one of Milly's poker nights and met all her crazy poker gals, as Mil called them. Milly had promised Steph it would be a fun night and Mil didn't let Stephanie down. She had a ball with all those crazy women.

Anne walked into the house, coming back from the store and knelt down to hug Ryan's German Shepherd, Rags. Ryan had forgotten to get celery for the stuffing and Brad, her other brother, had volunteered to get it. Brad had asked Anne if she wanted to go to the store with him on his bike. The excited glow she radiated made both Stephanie and Hunter smile. Anne was eating up all the attention she was getting from both new friends.

Stephanie could tell that Hunter and Brad were busy talking about their Harleys while drinking their beer. It made her feel good to see how well Hunter got along with her brothers. Those three guys were probably going to become good friends.

Stephanie walked in the kitchen where Ryan and Milly were talking away. Ryan had just taken the rolls out of the oven.

"Hey, Ry, would you like me to make the gravy?"

"Yeah, thanks, Steph, that would be great. Milly and I will put the food on the table while you're busy with the gravy."

Stephanie was content to just watch the gravy while she stirred. She heard someone walk in the kitchen, then hands slid around her waist. Only one person would do that and it made her smile.

Without even turning around, Stephanie commented.

"I'm glad you and my brothers are getting along."

"Yeah, it seems we have a lot in common. They seem like good guys and they also have a quirky sense of humor, like someone I know."

Hunter leaned down and kissed her on the cheek.

Just then Ryan and Milly came back into the kitchen.

"OK, make-out sessions are strictly forbidden in the kitchen," Ryan said. "especially right before we eat. God, I hope I don't lose my appetite."

Stephanie turned off the stove and wrapped an arm around Hunter's waist. She gave her brother the smart-ass grin that they knew and loved.

"Go wipe your nose, Ryan, your brain is leaking."

Brad had walked in seconds before Stephanie spoke and broke out into laughter along with the others.

Ryan shook his head while he laughed.

"You know I'll get you back for that one."

"You can try."

Milly calmed down from laughing and said.

"You know, you guys, you need to meet the people Hunter works with. They're as crazy as you. Hey, as a matter of fact we're having a New Year's Eve party and it would be a great time for the two of you to meet all of them."

Brad was the first to speak up.

"I'm game."

Ryan agreed.

Milly added.

"You are also welcome to bring a date."

Brad gave her a smile.

"I'll do that, thanks."

Ryan looked down and nodded.

"OK, Ryan, the gravy is done. Let's all put the rest of the food on the table. I'm starving." Stephanie said, as she handed Hunter the bowl of mashed potatoes.

Everyone grabbed something the rest of the food and went to the dining room.

They were all seated, but for some reason Brad had to get up a couple of times to get something. After the second time Ryan looked at Brad.

"Brad, would you sit down and give your brain a rest."

Which was the start of one of the best Thanksgiving dinners Hunter had ever been to.

When their stomachs were nice and full, they eagerly waited for the apple pie and pumpkin pie to cool off before they submerge into their desserts. All of them were desserts lovers and never went without.

CHAPTER THIRTY-TWO

Ryan got up from the couch to face Milly, who was sitting across from him on his favorite recliner chair.

"Hey, Mil, 1 want to show you the pond that I put in last summer. It has a forty foot stream along with it."

He held out his hand to help her up.

Hunter had never seen his aunt's face turn red as it did when she let Ryan help her up. He watched the two of them walk towards the door leading into the backyard and he again wondered about Stephanie's observation of his aunt and Ryan.

He glanced at Stephanie and noticed a cute little smirk on her face with her eyebrows high on her forehead. He wouldn't be surprised if Steph had the same thought as him.

But Brad seemed oblivious to what was going on between his brother and Milly. He was too busy channel-surfing, looking for a football game on TV.

Anne concentration was on something else and gave Hunter a concerned look and asked.

"Hunter, I know we talked about leaving Patches with Jake, but do you think Patches is going to be OK with us here and me not giving her her daily walk?"

"Oh, sweetheart, don't worry. Jake knows we were going to be gone all day and with him volunteering to stay at the house and plans to walk and feed Patches for you, not to mention give her all the attention she'd wants."

Anne's concern changed into delight.

"Patches loves Jake. I bet she's loving all the attention he is giving her."

That made Hunter smile.

"I'm sure of it Anne. I saw how Patches fell into his spell."

"What do you mean Hunter?"

Stephanie noticed how Hunter stepped into that one and decided to rescue him.

"You know what a nice and funny guy Jake is. Well, it's the good person in Jake that attracts Patches along with other animals. They have a keen sense and know when they come in contact with a good person."

"That's right. I remember how Patches just loved Jake. And you're right, he is a wonderful, funny guy. That makes me feel better. Thank you."

"You're very welcome, sweetheart."

Stephanie looked at Hunter and he gave her a thank you nod.

Brad heard the conversation and asked.

"Anne, you have a horse?"

"Oh yes. Hunter rescued her from being hit by a car on Highway One."

Brad looked at Hunter,.

"OK you can explain now."

Hunter told the whole story about Patches.

Brad was blown away.

"Wow, what a cool story. So now she's doing well and it's all because of you, Anne. That's quite a responsibility that you accomplished."

Hunter got the biggest kick out of how Anne accepted Brad's compliment and just said thank you.

Brad had an idea.

"Hey, you guys, when we go to your place during Christmas would you like me to give Patches a complete check-up? I'll be there anyway and it will save you some vet expenses."

Hunter liked that idea. He would call his vet to let him know that Brad would give Patches her next checkup. If there was something wrong Brad would write a report for him.

"Thanks, Brad, that would great. I'll get hold of Dr. Percy to let him know what's going on."

Anne looked confused.

"What is it that you do that would help Patches, Brad?"

"I'm a veterinarian like your Dr. Percy."

Now she was excited.

"You are! That's what I'm thinking of being."

Now Hunter was surprised.

"Anne, when did you decide this?"

"Since I've been taking care of Patches and since I love animals so much. I think it would be a perfect career for me."

Brad gave her a big smile.

"It definitely helps to love animals. If you do decide to pursue being a veterinarian, feel free to talk to me. I'll be more than happy to help you out."

Anne jumped up from where she was sitting and ran to Brad, giving him a hug.

"Thank you, Brad. That's wonderful. I wish your practice was in Boulder Creek though so I would be able to help you when the time comes."

"Well, you never know what fate has in mind. It may happen."

Now Stephanie was excited, thinking of *"what if's"*.

"You know you can also keep the practice you have now and have someone else run it while you move to our area. Oh, Brad, that would be a dream come true for me."

Brad knew he had put his foot in his mouth by making that statement.

"Oh boy. Sis, I'm not saying it's a sure thing, but you never know. To be honest I would love to move over there, but that's going to take a lot of planning and finding another building."

Stephanie now was gung ho on the whole idea of Brad living closer to her. Now that she was thinking about Brad moving closer to her, she had to think of a way to get Ryan over there too.

"Well, while you're deciding I'll look on the Internet and

talk to a broker and have them start looking for veterinarian practices who specialize in horses, which mean you're going to need some land also and a big building. Don't worry I know it won't be right away, but I'm still excited that you would even think about moving down there."

Anne was beside herself also.

"Oh Brad, please think about moving closer to us. That would be so much fun."

***

Anne reminded Brad so much of Stephanie when she was that age. He was drawn to Anne right away and could tell Ryan was the same way. They loved including their sister in whatever they did because she was able to keep up with them and she was fun to be with. Besides, she was one tough little cookie. Stephanie played some sports better than some of their friends.

He remembered their friends how they reacted when they first brought Stephanie to play tag football with them, but after playing the first quarter with her they soon shut the hell up. She was fast and was able to dodge a lot of them.

Boy, he had opened up a can of worms, but he'd been wanting to get closer to his siblings. He really missed them.

He wasn't going to say anymore about the move, but just maybe, we'll see. But in the back of his mind he'd get the ball rolling, knowing Stephanie meant what she said about looking for a place in there area.

He owned the building where his vet business was and didn't want to give it up, but knew he would probably have to hire another vet to help out his partner with the very busy business they deal with daily. His building was in a great location and definitely didn't want to let it go.

***

"Let's take it a day at a time, sweetheart." Brad replied. "Steph and I would need to do a lot of research before then, but I do like the idea."

Anne was content with that response.

"Oh good."

That's when Anne remembered the pies.

"Do you think the pies are cool enough now?"

Stephanie got up and started to walk off when she turned around and looked at Anne.

"Why don't we check them out? Who else is up for pie?"

Both Hunter and Brad answered with a yes. Both saying apple please, knowing they'd be back for their slice of pumpkin also.

Stephanie stopped again and asked.

"Who wants ice cream with that."

In unison they said, "I do."

Since Ryan and Milly were still outside, she left their slices on the counter. They were all busy enjoying the delicious apple pie when Ryan, Milly and the dog walked backed in.

Ryan saw what they were eating.

"Hey, you didn't wait for us."

Stephanie looked at Ryan with her smart ass smirk.

"Would you like some cheese and crackers to go with that whine?"

Milly broke out laughing.

Stephanie continued.

"Besides, we had no idea when you'd be back and our mouths were watering for dessert. Your apple pie is already on a plate and the pumpkin pie is cut up waiting to be eaten too, once I'm finished with this piece."

Brad said nothing, just grunted, nodding his head. The others were busy eating and enjoying what was left of their pie.

"OK, fine, Milly and I will get ours."

Stephanie yelled to them.

"Don't forget the ice cream."

Hunter had just finished his pie.

"Damn, that was really good. What kind of apple pie was that?"

Stephanie and Anne said together.

"Dutch Apple."

Obviously Brad was a slow eater because he was still eating, but again he grunted and nodded his opinion too.

No sooner had Ryan and Milly started to walk out of the kitchen when the other three waited to walk in the kitchen for pumpkin pie.

Ryan needed to add.

"Save some for us too."

"Don't worry, there's more than enough pumpkin pie. There's another one that just needs to be warmed. I'll put it in the oven now for you now."

"Thanks, sis."

All of them except Hunter and Stephanie walked out of the kitchen with their pies.

Once Stephanie finished placing the pie in the oven, Hunter grabbed her by the waist and gave her a longing kiss.

"God, I've been wanting to do that all day long."

"Me too. I miss your kisses."

"Do you really think Brad was serious about moving over our area?"

"It sounds like it. I'm so excited. But I know Brad won't jump into anything. He'll do a lot of research about our area and hopefully he will find a place. I can't wait for that to happen."

"That would be so cool. I really like your brothers and I can see why you love them so much. They sure have taken to Anne. I think it's probably because she reminds them of you when you were younger."

"Never thought of it that way, but maybe. We three were so close and had so much fun together. But you can't help to fall in love with Anne. There's something about her that you just can't help yourself loving. Besides you can tell she's going to be beautiful as she gets older."

"Ugh, don't remind me."

That just made Stephanie laugh as they walked back into the living room.

By the time Hunter and his clan left it was already 8:30 pm and Anne was getting anxious to see Patches. She had all of the next day to spend with Patches, but she wanted to give

Patches her nightly apple before she went to bed.

Milly was smiling as they drove off.

"That was so much fun. Your brothers are really nice guys."

Hunter and Stephanie quickly glanced at each other, holding back their smiles. They knew something might be going on between Ryan and Milly; time would tell.

It took about a little over an hour to get back to Boulder Creek. As soon as Hunter parked his truck Stephanie jumped out, knowing Anne wanted to get out of the truck to see her Patches.

Jake met them as soon as Hunter pulled in. Anne rushed over to Jake, hugging him and thanking him, then running off to see Patches.

"Hi guys, how was your visit?"

Stephanie reached into the truck and pulled out a large container of turkey dinner and both apple and pumpkin pie. She handed it to Jake.

"Wow, thank you."

Hunter figured Jake was hungry.

"Your welcome to eat it here while you tell us how your day went with Patches."

"Sure, no problem. Let's go in because this is making me hungry again.

Jake was too busy scarfing up his second dinner to talk, so Hunter asked.

"Hey, Jake, since you weren't able to go to Arizona to see your mom and sis, are you going over there for Christmas?"

Once Jake swallowed he said.

"Yep, I called them to let them know that Christmas would be the holiday I would be seeing them. Damn, all this food was good and now for dessert. Thanks, guys, for thinking of me."

"Well, you can thank Stephanie since I completely forgot about feeding your ass."

"Well, then, thank you, my Stephanie. That gesture was really appreciated."

Before Stephanie could reply Hunter said.

"Hey, there's no *my* when you say Stephanie, that word

belongs to me."

"Touchy, touchy, aren't we, *my* man. But don't forget if it wasn't for me you would still be making up you damn to-do list. So if anything I should be the only one, besides you and her siblings, to be entitled to say *my* when it comes to Stephanie. What do you think, Stephanie?"

"First of all, I'd be honored with that endearment from you and second what are you talking about Hunter's to-do list?"

Hunter moaned and Jake broke out laughing.

"Do you want me to explain or would you like the honors?"

Again Hunter moaned, then finally said.

"No way am I going to let you explain and blow it out of proportion, thank you very much. I'll tell her."

This whole time Stephanie was leaning against the counter, arms crossed with a questioning look on her face.

Hunter was standing next to her and he put his arm around her.

"Babe, after I met you my thoughts were consumed with you and to be honest it scared the hell out of me because it never happened to me before. So to keep from getting distracted with thoughts of you, I made a to-do lists to keep my mind and body preoccupied, which did help at times, it wasn't a hundred percent. Then idiot over there got us together with his plan, and I'm very thankful he did that."

Hunter lifted his chin towards Jake who was now busy eating his slice of apple pie.

Stephanie broke out laughing.

"So that's what all this was about? I remember Anne saying something about a to-do list when I fixed dinner for you guys and I also remember something being said the time we were at Henflings. And to be honest Hunter I was doing the same thing when it came to you. I thank my job because to do my job, I had to take my attention away from thinking of you. And let me thank you now, Jake, for the so called set-up of yours. I have no regrets."

Jake pushed the empty plate that had held his large slice of apple pie and grabbed for the large slice of pumpkin pie.

"You two are very welcome, even though I wasn't the only one who saw the sparks fly between you. I'm glad it turned out for the better."

With that said he ate a chunk of pumpkin pie as he moaned. '"Mmmm," nodding his head.

CHAPTER THIRTY-THREE

Thanksgiving holiday was over. It was Monday and the PanHead group were back at work. Jake had left for a meeting with the Planning Department, about the new building. Hunter was in the office working on the books. The others were busy working on a some bike, while Stephanie was in her office, busy designing. Her and Paula had just finished their break together. Business was booming, which meant more bikes in the shop. They all were looking forward to having more room to move around in, once the new building was finished. They all were so busy it left little time to bullshit while they worked. Time went by even faster.

A couple of bikes drove in with a roar. Spike wiped his hands on a cloth from his back pocket as he walked toward the two guys who had just arrived.

"Hey, Mike, Chris, long time no see."

Mike got off his bike and gave Spike a man hug.

"Good to see you too, man. I've been up north for a while and just recently got back."

Chris got off his bike and shook Spike's hand.

"One of the reasons we came by was to show you this. I wasn't sure if you read this magazine yet."

Mike pulled a magazine from his back pocket.

"Arlen Ness was being interviewed and was asked what he thought the next up and coming Harley shop would be and I'll be damned he said the PanHead Custom Harley Shop and

Repair."

Arlen Ness was a big name and a God amongst bikers of the world. The man and his shop were well known.

Spike was surprised.

"How would he know. He's never been here."

"Apparently it doesn't matter. You know how always throughout the day bikers come to this shop for some reason or another. Well, it seems Arlen has seen some of the bikes that PanHead has built and designed. Supposedly he liked them and was really impressed with whoever was doing the design work. I swear, bikers are like a bunch of little old ladies when it comes to talk'n Harley."

That made Spike laugh.

"Yeah, you are so right about that. Let me see what the magazine has to say."

Mike handed him the magazine, showing him Arlen Ness's article. While Spike was reading, Chris and Mike stood around admiring Rob's 48 Panhead, and talking to Rob and Paula.

Spike had just finished the article when Hunter walked out and waved Hunter over.

"What's up?"

"Read this and you will know why business has picked up."

Spike left Hunter to go back to work.

"Well, I'll be damned."

That was all Hunter could say as he read the article, smiling.

Hunter overheard Chris talking about the new designer that PanHead had and how word was going out about how good he was. Hunter had to laugh to himself. Apparently no one knew he was a she. Which was OK with him. The majority of those that asked about the new designer were given her last name Pierce. But no one ever asked what the first name was, so far. He knew it wouldn't be long before someone knows the truth and it would spread.

Hunter walked over towards Mike and Chris, shook hands and asked about the article. Mike was happy to repeat what he knew. Just then Jake drove up on his Harley. The greetings started all over again, with Hunter handing Jake the magazine.

Once Jake read the article he had a big ass grin.

"Well, I'll be damned."

Jake thanked Mike for bringing it over. Soon after Mike and Chris roared off. The rest of the day the group's spirits were high and they were all in an even better mood.

Worked ended and they were still talking about the article. Someone had put on some music and Rob grabbed Paula and started dancing.

CHAPTER THIRTY-FOUR

Christmas was getting closer and Hunter was still trying to figure out what he should get Stephanie for her present. He knew Anne would flip over the new saddle he had ordered and the present for his aunt was going to be special, a way to show his love and appreciation for all that she had done to help keep the family together. One item on her bucket list was to spend a month in Paris and he had arranged the trip. He knew that would be the perfect present for his aunt. He also knew she was going to flip. She always said that someday she wanted to start one of her novels in Paris. This would be her chance.

But Stephanie was another matter. Maybe he should talk with one of her brothers to see if they had any ideas, but he doubted they would. He had talked with Anne and they both decided that whenever Anne was around Stephanie, Anne would make sure to keep her eyes and ears open in hopes that Stephanie would mention something she wanted, without Anne having to ask. Anne was definitely all for the job. It was a silent game that she and Hunter would be playing.

Now that Stephanie was moved in, it was her turn to have her whole family over for Christmas. The celebration was going to be held at their place. Hunter was looking forward to meeting the parents of this wonderful woman.

The three of them decided to drive up Bear Creek Road to shop for a live Christmas tree. Since there were a number of tree farms up there they had no doubt that they would find one. Christmas was Stephanie's favorite holiday and Anne's too, so the two of them were humming with excitement. The two of them decided that when they arrived home they would decorate the tree first and then the inside of the house. On day two and three, they would start the baking. First they bake a variety of different of Christmas cookies. Then on day four they would pick three of their favorite cookies, with the majority ruling. Hunter was all for that, as long as he didn't have to do any of the labor.

Normally he and Anne bought a Christmas tree that was already cut down, so getting a live tree was a first for them. When Christmas was over they would plant it close to where the new shop was going to be.

Hunter realized what a positive influence Stephanie had been for Anne. He made it a point to do little things around the house, helping in some simple ways, but his favorite was that every night he was more than happy to show her how much she meant to him in their bed. His feeling for her just keep getting stronger.

It was also good to see Aunt Milly do activities that she had been wanting to do but chose not to. She had put her book touring on hold for so long that her agent thought she was kidding around when Milly told him she was ready to tour. So right now she was in San Francisco meeting up with her agent working on her up-in-coming tour date, starting at the beginning of the year, promoting the latest in her paranormal series, and would head to New York on the second week of January. She has won numerous writing awards for the series. Anne brought up the fact how different it had been not being able to see her auntie since she was gone a lot now. You could tell Anne was missing her. Again, thank goodness, Stephanie was here for Anne.

This was the fourth day and the last of the winning cookies were to be baked. Stephanie and Hunter went home for lunch. Their lunches usually ended up in bed, but today Stephanie wanted to finish baking the last batch of the cookies they that had won the vote. No sooner had she put the cookies in the oven then the phone rang. When Hunter heard the phone he knew their romp in the sheets was a no-go and he groaned. She heard his groan and knew what that was all about. She leaned into him kissing those fine lips of his.

"We have all of tonight to play."

Then she rushed to answer the phone.

She could hear Hunter groaning again.

CHAPTER THIRTY-FIVE

Ten minutes later Stephanie hung up the phone from talking to her brother, Ryan. She walked back in the kitchen where Hunter stood leaning against the counter as he ate a sandwich. Hunter noticed her shocked expression.

"Babe, what happened?"

"That was Ryan on the phone. He called to tell us that he will be moving over here."

"Are you serious! Although I think it's great idea. But what in the hell made him want to do that?"

"Yeah, I'm serious and believe it or not, I'm really excited, I'm just still a little surprised."

"What else did he say?"

"Well, he said he is being transferred to the CHP Aptos station in a few months. He wants to know if I know of a reliable Realtor. I asked him whereabouts over here would he like to live. He said anywhere between Boulder Creek and Aptos. He would be happy with a two-bedroom, two-bathroom place with some land around it."

"Wow, Was this a mandatory or voluntary decision? I have a feeling it's voluntary, I don't know why, although I am a little curious."

"Well, I think I know why." Stephanie said as she started to smile,"but what I tell you is just between you and me. Because if I'm right it's going to be a positive and I don't want to blow the situation up more than it is, for now."

"OK, sure, I won't say anything, just tell me. Now you've really got my curiosity going."

"Well, when we spent Thanksgiving at Ryan's I noticed how he was with your aunt and let me tell you, Hunt, he was not being the normal Ryan that I know and love. Remember how I told you how my brothers were pretty much horn dogs when it came to women? Your typical love'm-and-leave'm male type."

Hunter grunted his response.

She held her finger up halting him from saying anymore.

"Well, I noticed he wasn't coming on to Milly, like he usually does with women. It's just so weird. I have to say he was different. What I'm trying to say is, I think there was more than attraction with Ryan. You know, like that spark between us when we first met. Well, I have a feeling he felt that spark with Milly. But I'm not sure if Milly felt the same."

"Well, I'll be damned. I think you're right. I think there might have been some kind of spark with my aunt too. But before I tell you anything further I need to back up and explain my aunt. Since she has been helping raise Anne with me, she has always come across as calm, cool and collective when she dealt with men. She has always been confident in her looks and had put men on the bottom of her list until Anne graduated or I found someone. She told me when it was the right time she would meet the right man and not any sooner. But over at your brother's, I noticed something about Mil, but I just let it go, not putting any importance on it."

"OK, now you've got me curious."

"What I noticed was how she kept checking her makeup with her compact mirror and how she was a little more serious than I have ever seen her. So yeah, she was different also."

"Well I'll be damned. If we're right, fate sure does works in mysterious ways."

"Yeah, perfect timing."

"We can't let on to anyone, OK?"

He grabbed Stephanie towards him and kissed her.

"Sure, baby. But, at least the two of us can talk about it. You

know I really hope we're right because I would love to see
Aunt Mil with someone to love her."

"I agree, she deserves it."

Hunter looked up at the clock.

"Damn, we have to get back to work already."

"We always have tonight, my love."

She kissed Hunter on his cheek. The timer went off and she
took out the baked cookies and left them to cool.

Back at her desk, Stephanie was thinking about when she
had first moved out of her parent's home and was living in her
own apartment. Her memory went back to when she decided
to visit her brothers, who were living together right before
they graduated from college. And man, the women who were
always coming by or calling them, practically throwing
themselves at the two men. But that didn't seem to bother her
brothers. They ate it up and put all those willing women to
good use. It always bothered Stephanie that some of these
women didn't care if they made fools of themselves just as
long as they ended up being used by one if not both of her
brothers.

It always bothered her, but maybe these women felt so alone
that being with someone as fine as her two brothers made
them feel good, temporary though it was. One of her favorite
mottos was, *To each his own.* That made her understand
perfectly and be accepting. It was a little sad, though, if these
women were doing it out of desperation.

CHAPTER THIRTY-SIX

Work was over, but Stephanie wasn't planning on going home since she would be by herself anyway. Hunter and Anne were going Christmas shopping right after Anne took Patches for her daily afternoon walk and treat. This was a perfect time to go online and look up real estate office websites to see what they had to offer. She lucked out finding some property listings and printed them out for herself, then emailed them to Ryan, letting him know there would be more coming.

She was getting excited just thinking about having one of her brothers living closer to her. She wondered what was he going to do with that beautiful house that he owned in Pleasanton. *God ,it would be great to get Brad over here too.* After two hours of being on the computer and staring at the monitor, she needed to quit. Her eyes were blurring.

As she walked home she noticed a shiny dark gray Porsche, that she didn't recognize parked in the driveway. When she walked closer, the stranger's driver's side door opened and a gorgeous, tall, blond woman stepped out. Stephanie stood by the woman's car and waited.

"Hi there, my name is Jenny Kilman. I'm here to talk to Hunter, I work for the San Francisco Examiner and was hoping I could interview him. Besides, we go way back."

"Really? Well, he's not here at the moment, but I would be more than happy to give him your business card, if you have one."

"Oh, I sure do, sugar. Please tell him to give me a call anytime of the day or night. That number on the back of the card is for my cell, which I carry with me all the time."

Once blondie handed Stephanie her card, she turned back toward her car then stopped, turned around and said.

"Oh and please tell him that if he decides not to bother calling, I will just keep calling him and dropping by the house until I get my answer. I want that interview, plus I *really* want to see him."

She got into her car and drove off.

"Yeah, like that's going to happen." *Bitch. What in the hell did Hunter see in that woman anyway, besides a body that men would die for and a face that would put the majority of women to shame. No, not much... yeah right.* This time Stephanie felt her bitch meter reach to the red and she did not like the reaction.

Half an hour later, Hunter and Anne came home. Once Hunter parked the truck, Anne got out, rushing toward the barn, and yelled.

"Hunter, I'll be right in. I want to say good-night to Patches, OK?"

"Sure, Anne, but don't be too long, you've got school tomorrow."

"OK!"

Hunter walked in the house carrying some shopping bags. He yelled for Stephanie.

"Hey, baby, where are you?"

"In the kitchen."

He walked in to see Stephanie busy eating some leftovers from last night's dinner.

She looked up at him without smiling.

"How was shopping?"

Hunter had a feeling something was up with Stephanie. She was always smiling and at the moment she was being a little too calm and cool. What the hell was up?

"Well, I was able to get the majority of the presents for the group at work, plus Sam and Jason and even Aunt Milly. Come, I want to show you what I got."

Stephanie had another idea though.

"Before we go in the living room I wanted to tell you that you had a visitor this evening. Mind you, a very persistent visitor."

She told him about his blond bombshell.

As she mentioned the woman's name, Anne had just walked the kitchen at the same time.

Anne heard the name.

"Oh no, not the 'Wicked Witch.'

Hunter looked surprised.

"Anne, how in the world would you know who she was?"

"I was seven, Hunt, not a baby. I remember her. But what I really remember is, I overheard Aunt Milly calling that woman 'The Wicked Witch.' Because I think Aunt Milly didn't like her."

That made Hunter laugh.

"Yeah, you're right about that. The two of them clashed, big time."

He stopped smiling once he looked at Stephanie. He cleared his throat.

"Aaumm, she wasn't anyone special."

Anne looked puzzled.

"Then why did you go out with her, Hunter?"

This time when he looked at Stephanie, her eyebrows were raised. He gulped.

"Anne, honey, time for bed."

"OK, I got the hint, you guys need to talk. I'm going. Good night."

Stephanie gave her a smile.

"Good night, sweetheart."

"Babe, let's go in the living room and I'll explain everything about the 'Wicked Witch.'

He gave Steph, a smirk.

She was trying to hold back a smile.

"OK, let's go."

CHAPTER THIRTY-SEVEN

They sat down on the couch. Stephanie folded her arms in front of her and leaned back, waiting to hear what he had to say.

"That was a looonnng time ago, Stephanie. We dated a few times and *she* decided she was the one for me. But as you can see, she wasn't."

Hunter felt good now that he had explained. His reply made him feel confident he looked at Steph.

Straight face she replied.

"Keep going."

"That's it. It didn't work out."

"Obviously she was not one of your one-night stands. You said that's all you had. Am I right?"

"Well, yeah. I had forgotten about her."

Realizing he found an out, by telling her he had forgotten about her, he started to relax, just a bit.

"I see, go on."

Damn, that wasn't what he wanted to hear her say.

"Well, we went out two or three times, if that, but as you saw for yourself she was a little too much. It would have never worked out and I told her that."

"And..."

"And what?"

"Why did WW and your aunt dislike each other?"

"Apparently Aunt Mil knew what she was up to and didn't

like it."

"Let me guess. She was after a ring and didn't want Anne around."

"Yeah, hey, that was pretty good deduction."

"Well, she's back in your life and she's probably going to try to stir up trouble between the two of us."

"Let her try and see where she gets. Steph, I have no interest in her and I do not care if I ever see her again. I have a feeling she wants to interview me regarding the Arlen Ness article. I'm telling you now, I will call her back, just to get her off my back. But as far as the interview, she's going to have to talk to Jake, since he is the go-between man anyway. She has never meant anything to me and she still doesn't."

She gave him a smirk.

"That's what I figured, I just wanted to see what you had to say."

"Oh, you did, did you?"

Hunter stood up and picked her up in his arms. It was so fast that all she was able to say was, "Ummph."

Anne came in and laughed when Hunter threw Stephanie over his shoulders. Stephanie was too busy laughing and trying to breath at the same time. With Stephanie still over his shoulders, he made sure Anne was in her bedroom, still laughing, as he closed her door. Steph knew that for the rest of the night Hunter would show her what a naughty girl she was. He was also forgetting about locking the front door and forgetting to show her all the presents he had bought. It was obvious the presents would have to wait for tomorrow, since they had better things to do at the moment.

***

Two days later Jake walked in the office where Hunter was working on the computer. As he was typing, Hunter said, "Hey, man, what's up?"

"Just wanted to tell ya that I just got back from the interview with the woman you so affectionately called the Scorpion Queen."

"Oh yeah, how did it go?"

"That is one *hot* woman. I can't believe you two were an item a while ago."

"First of all, that woman couldn't exude warmth if she were on fire and secondly, we were never an 'item,' I only dated her two or three times and believe me, that was enough."

"Well, according to her, there was more between the two of you."

"Yeah, like space. And man, those few dates with her were enough for me."

"Damn, how could someone be that bad and look like that?"

"She's not that bad Jake. She'd give you the hair off her back."

That seemed to lighten the conversation and both guys laughed, which got Skip curious enough to walk in the office.

"What the hell are you guys laughing about?"

"We're just talking about that reporter who came by the other day."

"You mean the to-die-for blond bombshell, Jenny?"

"How in the hell do you know her name, Spike?" Jake asked.

"A couple of days ago, you went to answer the phone when guess who walked in but 'Miss Jenny, I am so fine,' herself. So while you were too busy talking business, she swayed over to me and started a conversation. Not only that, get this, she asked me out."

Hunter started to laugh and started imitating a priest, blessing him with his right arm in the air, gesturing the sign of the cross.

"May the Lord protect you."

That got Spike going.

"Damn you guys, what do you know that I don't?"

Hunter was smiling now.

"You are in for it, man."

"Why do I get the feeling you know something about this woman?"

"Yeah, I know something about her, but get it from Jake here. I still have work to do."

Jake walked up to Spike.

"Come with me and I'll be glad to fill you in."

***

The following Monday Jake noticed Spike looking haggard.

"What in the hell happened to you? You look like shit."

Spike grabbed a clean rag and placed it in his back pocket.

"That would be Miss Jenny."

"Are you shitting me? What the hell happened?"

"Thank God it was a one-time thing, which was last night. The woman is a control freak, not to mention that she has one of the biggest egos I've ever seen. She couldn't stop talking about herself and everything had to be her way, even in bed. We both decided that it wouldn't work out and I left this morning. So not much sleep."

"Well, if you get caught up on your workload today, then why don't you head for home and get some sleep. You make me tired just looking at you."

"Thanks, I'll do that."

CHAPTER THIRTY-EIGHT

Hunter, Stephanie and Anne were playing Scrabble, biding their time, anxiously waiting for Aunt Milly to finally come home from visiting her best friend, she hadn't seen in years, which had taken her to Chicago. Anne was beside herself. She couldn't wait to see her aunt.

"How much longer now, Hunter, before she gets here? I can't wait to see Aunt Milly."

"Not too much longer now, sweetheart. When I talked to her on the phone and mentioned to her that we wanted to pick her up, she asked if we'd mind if she let another friend of hers to pick her up, so she would be able to visit with her, and tell her about visit in Chicago. Mil said she would be home by six p.m. and by the clock it looks like another twenty-five minutes. So use some patience, just for a little more, OK?"

"OK."

Fifteen minutes later, Anne practically tackled her aunt as she got out of the car.

"Oh my love, I have missed you so much too."

Milly affectionately said while she hugged Anne. Lifting her head up at Hunter and Stephanie.

"It's so good to be home, you guys."

Stephanie looked just as excited as Anne.

"You're finally home. Between me and Anne, I don't know how we got through today. It's so good to see you back home safe and sound. I have a feeling you are going to be preoccupied with a certain person for the rest of the night."

"Yeah, it looks like it."

That was when Anne finally let Milly go. Milly bent down and gave her another kiss, then walked to Hunter and Stephanie, giving them both hugs and kisses. They all followed Milly toward her place, while Hunter carried her suitcases. Anne was going to sleep over and walked in the house with Milly. The two waved good-bye to Hunter and Stephanie.

Hunter was stoked. He was going to be alone with his lovely lady and he couldn't wait to get the evening started.

He locked their front door behind him and just stared at Stephanie's fine backside. *Damn she is fine.*

Stephanie turned back to face Hunter.

"Milly sure looks good, doesn't she?"

Hunter was unable to say anything. All he could do was give her that familiar hungry for you look.

"Oh no, Hunter, I know that look of yours."

She laughed as she started to walk backwards toward their room.

"You are a horny toad, Hunt, but you're not going to get any complaints from me and don't you forget it."

"Oh, no way, Renee, will I never forget, but you just remember that I'm definitely your horny toad and you are mine and only mine and don't *you* forget that.

"No way, Jose, will I forget."

She turned around and ran to the bedroom with Hunter right behind her.

The rest of the night was bliss for the two of them. They finally took a breather two hours later, only to eat, then headed back to the room and started the love fest all over again. Once they fell asleep they were clasped together in a blissful sleep.

Stretching and feeling oh so good the following morning, Stephanie reached out to the other side of the bed, hoping the person responsible for how she was feeling was still in bed with her. She was not disappointed.

Hunter was lying flat on his stomach and no covers, much

less sheets over him.

"Oh my, my, you are one fine piece of muscle."

Stephanie whispered, while she rubbed that behind of his.

"You keep doing that, sweetheart and I'll show you how fine I can be...again." Voice husky, but ready for another round.

"I'm sorry if I woke you, but, Hunter, you have the finest gluteus maximus I've ever seen and it seems my hand took control."

"Well, I'll be glad to turn over so you can take control of something else."

That got Stephanie laughing. She leaned down to kiss his neck.

"Aren't you hungry. Why don't you call the girls and see if they want to come over for breakfast, since I'll be the one cooking?"

At that moment Hunter's stomach betrayed him as it grumbled loud.

"Well, I was going to deny being hungry. Guess I can't now. So yeah, I'll go give the girls a call."

"And I'll go take a shower before I start cooking."

"Want company?"

"How about you call the girls and tell them to come over in an hour. Then come and join me."

Hunter got out of bed quickly and grabbed the phone, naked. Stephanie stood there staring at that man's body without realizing it. Once she came out of the trance, she went to collect her clothes to wear after her shower. Stephanie no sooner closed the shower door than it opened right back up.

"Wow, that was fast. What did they say?"

"Hey, I don't fool around when it involves you naked."

"Will they be over in an hour?"

"Yeah, they're coming. And speaking of coming."

He slid his hand down between her legs very slowly, only to go down on his knees and started kissing. Unfortunately they were only able to pleasure themselves just once before Stephanie insisted they had to stop, she needed to start cooking.

CHAPTER THIRTY-NINE

Anne walked in the kitchen with her plate and utensils and placed them in the sink and walked back in the dining room.

"Thank you, Stephanie, for the french toast and bacon. It was delicious. Hunter, after I help with the dishes I'm going to go see Patches."

"Sure sweetheart, I'll help you so Stephanie and Aunt Milly can visit for a little while."

The two siblings walked into the kitchen and started the cleanup.

When Stephanie heard the back door slam closed, she knew Hunter would be back any moment now. They decided to bring up Ryan moving over to their area and wanted to see her reaction.

No sooner had Hunter sat down than the phone rang. Stephanie answered it.

"Oh, hey, Ryan, did you like some of the real estate listings I sent you?"

Milly's eyebrows shot straight up in surprise.

"That's good. Milly just got back from her trip last night and we were going to tell her the news. Oh sure, I'll let you talk to Milly, hang on."

Looking at Milly, Stephanie said, "Hey, Mil, Ryan wants to say hi."

Hunter couldn't get over seeing his aunt blush and right now she was blooming. Milly took the phone from Stephanie, who had the biggest smile on her face, for she now knew Milly was feeling the same thing Stephanie felt when she met Hunter. She was excited for the two of them.

"Are you kidding me, you're moving over here? When?"

Hunter and Stephanie went into the living room to give Mil some privacy.

About ten minutes later, Milly came in the living room with a stunned look on her face.

"Did you guys know he's being transferred over here?"

"Yeah, we were going to tell you, but Ryan beat us to it.," Hunter replied.

Milly looked at Steph.

"He said you were going to help him find a place by sending more listings. If you need help I'll be glad to help since I am free for a couple of weeks."

"Oh, Mil, that would be great. I appreciate all the help you can give."

"Steph, do me a favor and e-mail me the listings you already sent him so I won't end up sending him duplicates, OK?"

"Sure, no problem, I'll head out to the office and send it to you now so you'll have all weekend to look through the different comps."

"Thank you, Steph. I should head home and start looking. I'll see you guys later. Love ya and thanks for breakfast, Steph."

Milly walked out.

"My pleasure, Milly."

Stephanie turned to face Hunter. They both had the biggest ass grin on their faces.

"Well, I'll be damned. Who'd have thought?"

"Yeah, I'm excited for them too."

"I think they make a nice-looking couple. I'm so excited. I can't believe my big brother fell hook, line and sinker, big time. Boy, fate is something else."

Hunter got closer to Stephanie and started to rub her back slowly and seductively.

"I'm sure glad fate threw us together. I haven't been happier with anyone until you. I'm counting my blessings.

Hunter was in the middle of giving Stephanie a passionate kiss when he heard Anne scream his name.

CHAPTER FORTY

The sun was shining on a unusually warm December day. Anne was happily talking to Patches and Blaze as they walked back to the barn from her afternoon bareback ride on Patches when she saw a raggedy-haired man hiding behind a tree next to the barn, watching her. She didn't like how mean he looked. *Did he want to hurt her? What if he did?* She didn't recognize him and didn't like how he made her feel. Right at that moment she was terrified. What she really wanted to do was run to the house, but leaving the two horses alone stopped her. Anne look ed away as she placed her hand on Patches, then glanced back toward where the stranger was. He was gone.

Anne hurried with both horses to the house, yelling for Hunter.

Hunter rushed out, with Stephanie right behind.

"What's wrong?"

Anne was shaking as she replied.

"I was walking the horses back to the barn when I saw this strange old man hiding behind a tree. He looked mean, Hunter. I don't know why, but he looked like he was mad at me and wanted to hurt me. Why do you think he was there, Hunter?"

"Sweetheart, do you remember what he looked like?"

He was an old man with angry eyes. His hair was scraggly. Looked like he hadn't combed it for days. Do you know who he is, Hunter?"

Hunter recognized the description of the former owner of Patches, but didn't want Anne to freak out.

"No, sweetheart, but I'll call the sheriff's just to let them know a stranger was trespassing on our property and watching you. Why don't you put the horses back in the barn and stay with them? I'll be right back. OK?"

"OK, Hunter, but what if he comes back while you're in the house? I'm scared."

Stephanie walked over to Anne and hugged her.

"I'll go and stay with you in the barn."

Anne grabbed Stephanie's hand and wouldn't let go.

"Anne, I want you and Stephanie to do something for me. OK, sweetheart?"

Anne was still shaking. "OK."

"I want you guys to place the board across the barn door to shut it from the inside. Do not open it for anyone until you hear me when I call out your name. OK?"

Hunter knew having her do that was overkill, but it would make Anne feel better and safer.

Tears were running down her face.

"OK, hurry Hunter."

With Stephanie's arm around Anne they walked to the barn with Stephanie holding Blazes rein, while Patches following right behind them. Once in the barn Stephanie put Blaze back in his stable with Anne doing the same for Patches. As soon as Anne placed the board across the barn door she rushed to Stephanie and wrapped her arms around her waist and held her tight. Patches had started neighing nervously before Anne released Stephanie and rushed to Patches to hug and calm her friend.

Hunter hung up the phone from talking to dispatch. Now he had to wait for the deputies to arrive. He knew they couldn't do anything but patrol the area, since there was no proof of who was behind the tree. He knew in the meantime he had to figure how to protect Patches during the day when everyone was gone. His mind was going blank with frustration.

Half an hour later two deputies arrived and took a report. Hunter mentioned his suspicions about Patches' prior owner, but the deputies told Hunter exactly what he had figured. There was nothing they could do until a crime was committed. They advised Hunter to purchase some type of security system or hire some security personnel to patrol their property. The cops suggested that he place a numbered lock on the barn door, with only Hunter, Milly, Anne and Stephanie knowing the code to get in, and also recommended a motion detector camera for his property. He was going to look into it. Soon the deputies left.

Hunter knocked on the barn door and called out Anne's name. The barn door opened and Anne rushed to Hunter, still shaking as she cried.

The deputies had asked to speak to Anne, but being too upset and still crying, she was no help.

Hunter wrapped his muscular arms around Anne's waist as her arms circled around him and she leaned into him.

"Who was that man, Hunter? He looked like he was mad at me. Were the cops here? Are they going after that man?"

Having Anne go through this frightening experience and not being able to do anything about it pissed him off.

"Sweetheart, I don't want you to worry about anything. I've talked to the deputies and it's going to be taken care of. Anne, it's important that you let me take care of this. The more you know, the more it will keep you upset and I don't want to see that. So let me handle it, OK."

"OK, Hunt ,OK."

Seeing the energy drain out of Anne, Stephanie rushed to her.

"Honey, you're exhausted. Let's get you ready for bed."

All Anne was able to do was nod. Stephanie put her arm around Anne's shoulders and they started walking toward the house.

Hunter grabbed an heavy long-neck lock to secure the barn door temporarily until he ordered the security system tomorrow.

The next morning Hunter called his old biking budding from his younger days, John Tanner, who worked with the Los Angeles Police Department, Hollywood Precinct, Homicide Detective Division. Tanner told Hunter the make and model of the security system and locks he owned himself. Since Tanner recommended the specific system, then that was what Hunter was going to get. He called the Security & Lock Company and they were going to send the package in the next day's mail.

Two evenings later Hunter was able to take a deep relief breath now that the cameras and lock were setup and working. He would sleep well that night.

CHAPTER FORTY-ONE

Christmas had finally arrived. Stephanie's brother, Brad had picked up their parents at the airport on his last day of work, before his vacation, which would last till the first week of the new year. They all loved their get togethers and from what her brothers has learned from being with Hunter, Milly and Anne it's going to be fun get together all over again.

Stephanie was so excited. Later in the day her whole family would be back together. Finally, after being apart from her parents for a whole year she'll be able to introduce them to Hunter and his family. She had a feeling her parents were going to fall in love with all three of them, especially Anne. Stephanie knew that her dad had a special place in his heart for his only daughter and that her mom missed their get-togethers and the girl talk they use to have. When they met this sweet, loving girl, they were going to fall in love. Hell, her own brothers had fallen for Anne.You couldn't help it. Anne with her pleasant disposition and lovely personality, – yeah, her parents were goner.

The house was filled with a cinnamon scent, as the christmas tree lights blinked away. A fire was started in the fireplace to take over the morning chill as the flames reached out. Christmas music was playing and would be played throughout the day.

There was a knock on the door with Milly letting herself in, holding a big bag filled with christmas presents in one hand

and a steaming cup of hot cocoa in the other.

"Merry Christmas everyone!"

Anne and Stephanie wearing robes over their sleepwear were standing by the stereo and looked toward the front door. Anne went to her aunt and took the bag from Milly to give her a careful hug, not wanting her to spill her drink.

"Merry Christmas to you too, Auntie."

Once Anne finished her hug she eagerly took the large bag and placed all the presents under the christmas tree.

Stephanie walked over to Milly greeting her with a hug.

"Merry Christmas to you too. I'm so excited for you to meet my parents."

"After meeting you siblings, I want to see who were responsible for raising three terrific kids. I remember you saying they're a kick to be with. I can't wait."

"Yeah, it's going to be fun all day long."

Milly noticed Hunter wasn't around.

"Where's Hunt?"

Anne stood up took her aunts hand.

"He didn't want to come out in his pajamas, so he's taking a shower."

Stephanie inwardly laughed knowing Hunter never wears pajamas.

Hunter walked in the living room, rubbing his hair with a towel.

"I thought I heard you Auntie. Merry Christmas."

Milly gave Hunter a big hug, damp hair and all.

"Oh, Merry Christmas to you sweetheart. Which are we going to do first, open presents first or have breakfast?"

Milly knew that got Anne's attention.

"Open presents!"

Hunter spoke up.

"Let me put this towel back in the bathroom then let's open some presents!"

Anne was in charge of handing out the presents. It was planned to give Aunt Milly her present from Hunter, last.

When Stephanie opened her present from Hunter, she was

totally shocked. He had given her a 15" Apple Mac Book Pro, that had the latest Adobe Photoshop program and the same for Adobe Illustrator program installed, plus the design program she had at work, so she could do some work at home. Hunter had also bought her an Epson Printer. She was so stoked.

As for her present to Hunter, she had found the exact dark brown leather jacket that he had now. She had searched the Internet to find the company that made the jacket and was happy they still carried them. She knew it was his favorite, so she figured he would be able to wear the new one on special occasions, while he could still wear the old worn-down one any other time. Hunter loved the idea since he was getting a little concern his old one would wear out.

Anne's smile went from ear to ear when Hunter told her that he had forgotten one more present he had gotten for her and got up and went to his bedroom.

Anne's eyes bugged out when she saw Hunter carrying a beautiful tan leather saddle. She jumped up and ran to him.

"Thank you Hunter. Oh, what a beautiful saddle. When can we put it on Patches?"

"How about after we eat breakfast and clean the kitchen?"

"I can't wait. Thank you again, Hunter."

Anne knew there was one last box under the tree and handed it to her aunt.

"This is the last present and this one's for you Auntie."

Stephanie was so happy to witness was Aunt Milly's reaction of Hunter's present.

Milly was busy opening a small box big enough to hold gloves. When she saw what was inside and read the simple note saying *This is my way of thanking you for all that you've done for us* taped on top of the open-end round trip tickets to Paris, France, she was so shocked that she covered her eyes and sobbed.

Hunter got up and sat next to his aunt and wrapped his arms around her. With Anne following suit. Stephanie was too busy crying to move. She did notice Hunter too was also touched. When he finally looked up at her, she noticed his eyes shining with tears. Once the three of them released each other, Stephanie got up to hug Milly.

"Well, I'd say you were surprised,"

Steph said as she wiped her own eyes.

Milly was wiping her eyes with a tissue that Anne gave her.

"You know, Steph, I remember a long time ago that going to Paris and writing my next novel was one of my dreams. When I saw the tickets that said Paris, France, then read Hunter's note, I just lost it. He made one of my dreams come true."

"God, Mil, it was such a tender moment. I couldn't move since I was too busy crying."

That statement made everyone laugh and relax.

Hunter walked over to Stephanie and stood behind her to wrap his arms around her waist.

"This is some great Christmas, Hunter, don't you think?"

"Yeah, babe, I have to agree."

***

A couple of hours later they were all cleaned up and dressed. Stephanie and Milly in the kitchen prepping the turkey to be put in the oven. Milly was going to make her homemade dinner rolls that were to die for. Hunter had bought a keg of Heineken beer, along with dutch apple pie and pumpkin pie from Costco. Anne had finished making the rest of the cookies, so she was now in the barn with none other than her Patches and Blaze giving them their treats.

When her clan arrived Stephanie was so excited. She rushed outside to hug her parents. They arrived in two cars. The parents in one and the boys in the other.

Don and Patty Pierce finally was introduced to the special man in her life, along with his aunt Milly, while Anne was still in the barn, busy with Patches.

Don Pierce shook Hunter's hand.

"I have heard nothing but positive from all three of my kids and it's a pleasure to meet the special person in my daughter's life."

Hunter knew he was going to like Steph's parents. If the parents were anything like their kids then he couldn't have been happier. Although it really was the other way around.

Once Don finished shaking hand with Hunter, Patty hugged Hunter and whispered in his ear.

"Thank you for making our daughter so happy."

As she let go of him she said louder.

"I'm so glad to meet you and the rest of your family. I'm guessing this lovely woman is your Aunt Milly?"

Milly walked closer to Patty and gave her a hug.

"Nice to meet you, Patty. I have to say, you should hear Stephanie's voice light up when she talks about you guys. I feel like I already know the two of you."

Don was next to meet Milly. A big guy that he was, as he gave her a bear of a hug.

"I even heard about you and let me say it's a pleasure to meet you."

That's when Ryan tapped his father on the shoulder.

"OK, dad. It's my turn now to greet her."

Milly blushed as Ryan gave her a longer than normal hug.

Brad shook Hunter's hand and hugged his sister.

"Hey sis. Where's the food?"

This was not a surprise. Brad had a bottomless pit of a stomach and always brought extra, because of him. What pissed her off, the guy never gained weight.

"Don't worry Brad. There's appetizers already out waiting for you."

"Oh goody. Hey all, let's go inside."

Everyone was still talking to each other as they walked in the warm scent-filled room.

CHAPTER FORTY-TWO

With all the introductions done, with the exception of Anne, it didn't take long for everyone to start enjoying themselves and relax. Both Hunter and Steph noticed how Ryan zoomed in on Milly and hadn't left her side. She was trying not to look too interested, but from the way Mil kept sneaking glances at Ryan, they most certainly could tell.

Stephanie noticed how all the guys were sitting around her dad as Hunter asked him about his experiences as an airline pilot. Ryan and Brad were also contributing to the storytelling, and Hunter got a kick from all the stories being told. The men in her family had liked and accepted Hunter and Milly wholeheartedly.

Annie finally came in from being with Patches to meet Stephanie's parents, giving Ryan and Brad a big hug.

She was introduced to Stephanie's parents and gave them a hug too, telling them how lucky she was to have Stephanie as Hunter's girlfriend and her best friend. That got her a big hug from Stephanie. Stephanie could tell her parents were already smitten with Anne.

Anne was excited for everyone to see her Patches. She looked at Stephanie's parents and brothers.

"When you have time, I want you all to come and meet my Patches. Hunter rescued her and we have been taking care of her ever since. Now she is beautiful."

Proud as he could be, Hunter explained.

"Don't let her fool you all, she was the only one who took Patches under her wing and cared for her. Now Patches is not only a beautiful healthy filly, but a horse that adores Annie and rightly so."

Annie spent time talking with everyone in the living room, getting to know Stephanie's parents and laughing along with them. She offered to get everyone their drinks and with Hunter's help she brought out more snacks for all to munch on before dinner.

Brad walked over to Annie and put his arm around her.

"How about we go and see Patches? You can show a couple of us at a time so your Patches doesn't get nervous seeing so many people at once. I'll go first."

"Good idea, Brad."

Annie replied.

"I think she would get a little nervous with a lot of people. You want to go now?"

"Sure, let's head out. I brought my medical bag to give her an exam liked we talked about at Thanksgiving."

"Oh yeah, that's right. Thank you, Brad, for remembering."

Don Pierce stood up and asked.

"Would you mind if I tagged along to meet your Patches also?"

"Of course not. Patches would be fine with another person there."

Anne explained. She grabbed Don's hand and the two of them walked to the barn with Brad behind them. Stephanie knew that Brad would give Patches a thorough exam and was glad her brother had remembered that he offered to look Patches over. It didn't matter where he went, he always took his foldable medical bag.

Stephanie could tell her father was smitten with Anne, as her brothers were. She bet within a couple of years Anne and Patches would be spending summers in Colorado with her parents. She knew her mother was going to grow attached to this delightful young girl. She also knew by watching how Anne reacted to her dad that it was only a matter of time before Anne would fall in love with Stephanie's mom.

A few hours later most of the group were in the garage as Stephanie showed off Pearl to them.

The guys in her family all wanted to take it for a ride. Don fell in love with Stephanie's bike and made it a point to plan a run with Hunter and his boys before he and his wife had to leave. Ryan, on the other hand, had an idea, so he decided he was going to be the last to ride Pearl. As soon as it was his turn as he got on the bike, but before he rode off he turned his upper body around and called for Milly.

Sticking her head out the door she yelled.

"Yeah?"

"Why don't you take a break and come take a ride with me?"

Red-faced, she replied.

"I was just going to start setting the table."

"Well, I'll make you a deal. If you come riding with me, when we get back, I'll help you set the table. What do ya say?"

"Oh, OK, give me a minute, I'll be right back."

Milly walked out, putting her jacket on. She sat herself behind Ryan and wrapped her arms around his waist.

As they took off Hunter said with a big ass-grin on his face.

"Well, we might as well go in. Those two might be awhile before they come back."

As the group started to walk toward the house Brad had a look on his face that said Hunter was talking in a foreign language.

"Why do you say that?"

Don rolled his eyes at Hunter. Hunter figured Don knew something was starting up between Ryan and Milly. It seemed like just Brad was out in the cold of ignorance.

Hunter replied.

"Well, Ryan wants Milly to show him the area he will be moving to eventually."

"Oh."

Was all Brad said.

Don shook his head as he walked behind Brad. He looked at

his daughter.

"That is one sweet ride, sweetheart and that simple design really brought out the bike. You did good."

"Thanks Dad. I sure love how she rides and I agree, she is a beauty."

Anne had come back in from walking Patches and Blaze and asked if anyone wanted to play a board game. Stephanie, Patty and even Don wanted to play and they chose to play the game, Sorry.

It was Stephanie and Patty versus Anne and Don. They would play in teams of two with the winners winning two out of three games. It was decided the losers would have to put the leftovers in containers, rinse the dishes and put them in the dishwasher, your basic kitchen cleanup.

During the game Hunter took Brad to show him the shop and then the blueprints of the new addition to the PanHead shop they would eventually have.

The two guys had just walked back into the house when they see Don and Anne excitedly giving each other a high five and hugging.

Hunter couldn't help but smile.

"I guess we know who the winners are."

"Damn right, we socked it to them, didn't we, Anne?"

Anne was having a blast with these people.

"That's right. Now after dinner I can go straight to see Patches. Thank you, Stephanie and Patty."

Stephanie had to laugh. This was how it was growing up in her family. Sunday-night board games always were a major part of what kept them all close, making sure they all had fun. The winner of the game would get to pick his or her favorite game, with all wanting to play. When the boys started high school the game nights didn't happen as often, but they had the fun memories to hang on to.

Stephanie and Patty were in the kitchen when they heard and saw her Pearl arriving and being driven back into the garage.

CHAPTER FORTY-THREE

Once in the house Ryan made it clear that he and Milly were now in a relationship. He had his arm around her and in front of everybody, he bent down and gave her a soft kiss on the lips, letting everyone know they were now an item.

Stephanie broke out laughing when she saw the shocked expression on Brad's face.

"When did this happen?"

Brad asked as he wiggled his index finger back and forth between Ryan and Milly.

Don laughed along with the rest of them. It seems like even Patty knew something was up with those two.

Stephanie shook her head at Brad.

"Damn, Brad, sometimes you make a black hole look bright."

That got the house roaring.

"Hey, how was I suppose to know?"

Brad looked at his mom.

"Don't tell me you knew?"

"No, my love, you are right, I didn't know. I noticed something was going on between the two and I thought it was wishful thinking on my part. But what I want to know is how could you *not* notice?"

All Brad was able to come back with was, "Uhhh."

Which only got the group laughing again.

Dinner was now ready. Ryan and Milly finished setting the

table, Patty and Steph started putting the food on the table and Hunter got everyone their drinks.

Dinner was delicious and Milly's homemade rolls were a hit. They all talked about Ryan's moving to Boulder Creek and razzing him about how once he met Milly he had to find some excuse to move over here. Not once did he deny any of it. Besides, he was too busy scarfing down Milly's rolls to say anything. All he did was nod in agreement while chewing on his roll.

***

Dinner was over and it was late in the evening. Stephanie's parents were now back at the cottage they were renting, while Brad was lying down on their couch in the living room watching T.V. As for Ryan, he had gone to stay with Milly. Anne was so exhausted from the big day she had she'd fallen asleep, with her head on Stephanie's lap as they all sat around in the living room after dinner.

Stephanie and Hunter were in their room getting ready for bed.

"God, I just loved today. It was so much fun being around my family and having them finally meet you, Annie and Milly."

"It was fun. You have a great bunch in that family of yours."

"That was so funny how Brad reacted with Ryan and Milly."

"He reminded me of Rob, when it comes to being the last to find out. I saw you turn around laughing and I almost broke out laughing too, once I noticed Brad's expression. But enough of talking, my sexy little chica, I have something else in mind to do right now."

Laughing, looking at Hunter, Steph said.

"Oh, I bet you do, Poncho. Let the good times roll."

***

It was the day after Christmas, Stephanie's parents and brothers would be staying till the 27th of December. Today her dad got his way and took Pearl out for a ride. Hunter rode his Harley and Brad was on a borrowed Harley. The three of them went riding up Highway Nine, heading to San Francisco. But

Ryan stayed behind. He had other things to do with Milly, as you can imagine.

Stephanie, her mom and Anne went to Capitola Village. Steph knew her mom loved quaint places and Capitola Village was quaint. Plus the beach was right there, since Annie had asked to go to the beach also. The three of them had lunch at one of the restaurants, then did some window shopping until they decided to sit on the beach and watch Annie run in the water. They couldn't have picked a better day to visit Capitola. The weather was so weird. It was like it was springtime, 77 degrees , even though it was still winter.

Since this was her parent's last day before they had to head back to Colorado, her dad had talked the guys, minus Ryan, into going to a San Jose Sharks game, especially since they were playing against Colorado Avalanche. Stephanie had to laugh. Her dad was like a little kid going to the circus. He was a big-time hockey fan and didn't get to go to any games at home, since he would have to travel three hours each way, so this was a big treat for him.

It was close to dinner when the girls arrived home. The three of them enjoyed eating Hearty Heros, requested by Anne, then Anne and Patty went horseback riding around their huge yard. Stephanie decided to get to know her new laptop was busy playing on her computer, relearning how to use the complicated Adobe Photoshop program.

Stephanie couldn't have asked for more a perfect holiday as this last one. Having someone special, besides her family, to celebrate the holiday with only added to her happiness. She loved how her relationship with Hunter has been growing and she doesn't have any second thoughts about how her feelings for him were stronger. She was the lucky one.

It was time to say their goodbyes. Everyone was hugging and kissing each other. Stephanie wasn't surprised when Don and Patty brought up to Anne that they wanted her to come to Colorado someday and stay with them, maybe for the summer.

Anne was beside herself when they also said Patches was

also invited. She loved the idea of going to Colorado to visit. Don told her that when the time came he and Patty could either drive back here to Boulder Creek and pick her and Patches, taking back with them one of Hunter's horse trailers, or Hunter and Stephanie could take her and Patches to Colorado and visit for a few days and Don and Patty would take her home at the end of summer. Anne was already looking forward to the visit, hoping it would come sooner than later.

Ryan and Milly finally walked out of her place. Ryan held his tote and had his other arm around Milly's shoulder. Patty and Don gave their goodbyes to Milly while Ryan and Brad did the same to Hunter and his group.

CHAPTER FORTY-FOUR

Stephanie and Hunter were back at work for the next few days until the New Year's Eve. They kept reminiscing about the great time they had had with both families. Stephanie could tell Ryan was knee-deep in love. The two love birds had never left Milly's place until it was time for Ryan to go. She was happy for those two.

She was now looking forward to the New Year's Eve party and was glad she would be able to see her brothers again since they planned to come to the party. This time Brad had decided he was going to stay at one of the cottages his parents had stayed at in Boulder Creek, but hopefully with a date. And everyone knew where Ryan would be staying.

***

A few days later Stephanie worked late to finish an order. She no sooner walked into the kitchen when Hunter and Milly came rushing in from the back door with Hunter holding an unconscious Annie in his arms .

"My God, what happened?"

Hunter laid Annie on the couch. Milly hurried to be next to her.

Hunter went to Stephanie and led her to the phone.

"Patches is missing. From what I could see, not without resistance from Patches and probably from Anne. I think Annie got in between Patches and whoever was taking her and was knocked out. I need to call the police and an ambulance."

Right away Stephanie remembered Anne's dream. Stephanie ran into the bathroom to get a wet washcloth and handed it to Milly. Milly looked up at Stephanie, her face was dripping with tears.

"Annie probably caught whoever was taking Patches. The barn door was wide open with Anne going in and out. I'm guessing when she walked back into the barn she must have confronted the horse-napper and tried her best to stop him. Now she has this big knot in the back of her head."

Dashing to the kitchen, Stephanie said. "I'm going to get some ice to put on that knot."

Ten minutes later two sheriff's patrol cars and an ambulance were parked in front of the house.

Since the lump behind Anne head was a lot bigger than they expected, the paramedics wanted to take her to the hospital. Milly went with the ambulance, with assurance from Hunter and Stephanie that they would be there after the cops left.

Talking to the deputies, Hunter couldn't help but feel this whole situation had something to do with the former owner of Patches.

"I think the former owner is responsible for this."

With deputy number one responded.

"Why would you say that?"

"A while back my sister saw a strange man in our yard glaring at her and scared the shit out of her. I filed a report with you guys. Her description of the guy sounded a lot like Patches' former owner. Let me get the report number for you."

Hunter went to the desk in his room and brought the report to the deputy.

Once the deputy read the report, he called in for another patrol car to head out to the abuser's house.

Half an hour later the patrol officer who went to the former owner's house called in and said there was no sign of truck, horse trailer, or owner.

An BOLO (Be On The Lookout) was sent out throughout the area, heading north, south and east. The police thought it would be unlikely the thief would be heading west taking a horse on a boat. What they had on their side was a chopper, which was now heading east towards Tracy. The California Highway Patrol was also on alert.

It just so happened that the KSBW news chopper was listening in on the police scanner and called to let them know they were heading south toward Watsonville and would notify them if they came across a truck pulling a horse trailer.

Stephanie and Hunter spent an hour tensely waiting. Then Hunter heard the dispatch from NetCom call in and tell the officer that the KSBW chopper had spotted a truck with a horse trailer heading south at King City. It didn't take long for the CHP to pull the truck over. It was confirmed that the truck was owned by Patches former owner, with Patches in the trailer.

Hunter offered to go get the horse. He and Stephanie couldn't get out of the house fast enough. As soon as the cops left they drove off to get Patches. While Hunter drove Stephanie texted Milly to tell her what was going on and where they were going. She said she would let Anne know once they got Patches.

Ten minutes later Milly called them, so relieved that Patches had been found. She told them that the doctors wanted to keep Annie till later that evening just to keep an eye on her, just to be safe. They had given Anne a mild sedative because once she became conscious she remembered what happened and she broke down, still upset about Patches. But she was now asleep. Milly couldn't wait till Annie woke up to tell her the good news.

Two and half hours later Hunter and Stephanie finally arrived in Kings City. Apparently the cops had put the suspect in the patrol car while one of the officers drove the truck and trailer to the largest, closest parking lot they could find; one of them called Hunter to give him the directions to their location.

They finally arrived and Hunter parked his truck and trailer, the two of them jumped out and rushed to where the CHP officers were standing. Once Patches former owner saw Hunter he started yelling from the backseat of the patrol car.

"That's my horse! You took that horse from me! You give me back my horse!"

One of the officers turned around to talk to the old man.

The second officer gave Hunter a rundown on all that had happened. Hunter asked if he could go to Patches. The officer agreed.

Hunter opened the door of the thief's trailer and heard Patches nervously neighing. When the filly heard Hunter's quiet voice, she tried to turn her head to get a good look at him, but to no avail. As soon as Hunter got close he started to rub her back as he talked softly to her. When Patches was finally able to look at him she started neighing again, as if she was excited to see him. She rubbed her head against Hunter.

Hunter just stood there hugging this beautiful filly. Tears ran down his face. Patches had become an important part of the family. Too important to lose. At that moment the realization of what all had happened hit him. He and the horse stood close, hugging each other in their own way for about five minutes.

Once Hunter calmed himself he turned around and saw Steph was standing nearby.

"Steph, come on up and take my place. I need to talk to the officer."

Stephanie walked into the trailer with shameless tears running down her face. Not saying anything to Hunter, she squeezed his bicep as he passed by her. She started to talk to Patches, who right away moved in closer as she talked to this special filly. Both of her arms were wrapped around Patches neck as Stephanie rubbed the filly's neck. While Steph was softly talking to Patches, the horse bent her head and leaned against Stephanie's shoulder, not daring to move from the love and assurance she was receiving.

It was close to a five-hour round trip and they were now headed back to Boulder Creek. Aunt Milly had called and said that Annie was finally awake and released.

The doctor had told her Anne had a mild concussion and needed to move slowly and to expect some headaches. Milly told them her friend was taking the two of them home and she would see them at the house.

Good thing Milly had called to say they were getting a ride home because it was 2 a.m. when Hunter and Stephanie finally arrived home. They were both beat but arriving home picked them up.

Slowly walking out of the front door, Milly led Annie outside. Annie was already crying. Patches wouldn't stop neighing when she recognized Anne's voice.

Hunter led Patches out of the trailer as Annie slowly walked toward her filly. When Patches and Annie got close enough, they all could hear Annie.

"Oh, Patches, I'm so sorry you got scared."

Patches nod her head and neighed, then lowered her head against Annie's cheek.

As long as Annie moved slowly Hunter let her lead Patches back into the barn. Hunter fed Patches and they all stayed until Annie gave Patches her nightly treat. When they were back in the house, exhaustion took over. Once Annie was tucked in and Milly left for her place, Hunter and Stephanie changed and flopped on the bed, falling right to sleep.

The next morning Hunter checked the video from the security camera. There on the screen was the former owner backing in the trailer behind the barn, and sneaking into the barn. When Anne walked in on him, the camera showed her hitting the old man and then being pushed away. She fell, knocking her head on one of the stalls. He couldn't believe the balls this old man had to try to take the horse away. He didn't get it. The old man starved the horse, yet he wanted her back and what for, to starve it again? No, probably to sell it, now that the horse look good.

The next day at PanHead, Hunter told the group what had happened, leave it to Jake to bring Anne some flowers after work. Anne was charmed like every other woman. Jake stayed and had dinner with them that night.

CHAPTER FORTY-FIVE

Anne's headaches were mild now, if she had any at all and like everyone else, she was looking forward to the party. She was able to move a lot faster than she was three days ago. She couldn't wait till her girlfriends arrived.

This New Year's Eve was a unusually perfect night for a celebration. With a new year approaching, no rain and the night air surprisingly warm enough not to be bundled up. Hunter's house was filled with cheer and laughter. Hunter was feeling good and excited. He had something planned before the New Year. His friends and loved ones were laughing while one of the jokers within the group was keeping them all entertained. Even Anne was in her element. She and her friends were too busy with themselves to wonder what the older folks were doing. He watched as the young girls, each with a carrot or apple in her hands, headed to the barn.

Right now there were two poker tables with eight players at the table, trying to out do one another. The winners of each table would play the other for the pot. His Aunt Milly wasn't kidding when she said that her poker gals' are sharks. There were a couple of those sharks at each of the table and it looked as if their piles of poker chips were higher than the rest of the players'. At one of the tables Jake whooped it up since he had just won a round, while his date stood behind him with her hands on his shoulders.

Stephanie had lost all her chips. She left the table and

walked toward Hunter.

"God, Hunt, it's been a blast tonight. Looks like everyone is enjoying themselves too. Have you noticed that right now Spike is a little too preoccupied with Cassandra over in the corner to even want to play cards? Although I can see why."

Stephanie had met Cassandra at one of Milly's poker nights with the girls and she considered Cassandra the quiet one compared to the other extroverted ladies. She liked her right away, since she had been the type of person who kept to herself pretty much, until she met Paula. But right now it looked like Spike was smitten with this attractive, petite, pale red headed woman.

"Yep, I have to agree with you, Steph. Spike looks smitten. I noticed that when he was introduced to the poker girls he zoomed straight to Cassandra. I don't think he wanted to take the chance of someone else entertaining her since Josh and Sam also came here without dates."

His Aunt Milly and Ryan were sitting next to each other at one of the tables. Ryan was displaying his affectionate nature by holding Milly's hand, hugging her and giving her tender kisses as they played poker. It looked like he was too busy paying attention to Milly to care if he won or lost, while Milly's stack of poker chips was increasing in height.

The poker game continued on for about another hour. The final winners each ended up winning over two hundred and seventy-five bucks. The winner at table one was one of Milly's poker gals, Sharon. She would play against Rob, the winner at table two.

Hunter noticed Anne and her friends walking back into the house. He gave Anne a nod, letting her know it was time. Before the party, when the two of them were in the barn, Hunter had brought up an idea to her to see what she thought of it. Anne was gung-ho for it. She led her friends closer to the other guest and Hunter asked for everyone's attention.

Once the room was quiet Hunter turned to Stephanie, looked into her eyes, and said.

"Stephanie, I never thought I would feel as fulfilled as I do since I've met you. I would love to continue on with you at my side for the rest of my life. Will you marry me?"

Stephanie was shocked. Her hands covered her mouth while tears freely flowed from her eyes.

"Oh, Hunter, yes, definitely."

She reached out and wrapped her arms around his neck and they kissed. Well, more like a make-out session.

Anne rushed over to hug them, only to have Hunter pick her up. The three of them hugged each other. The rest of the party came over, giving their congratulations.

Aunt Milly, with tears in her eyes, couldn't have been happier. She hugged Stephanie, telling her she was a dream come true for her nephew. Ryan picked up his kid sister, saying he was proud of her and telling her she did real good job picking her future mate, only to look at Milly with desire and hope in his eyes, for he had plans with that woman too.

The clock hit midnight and everyone started to sing "Auld Lang Syne."

Stephanie wrapped her arms around Hunter's neck as she looked into his eyes.

"I promise you our life together will be a wonderful adventure and no matter what, I will always be by your side in whatever and wherever our life takes us. Thank you, Hunter, for making me so happy. I love you."

"I couldn't have said it any better, sweetheart. I love you too."

In the background you could hear Rob shouting "Let's the games begin!" The poker game between the two players had begun.

THE END

ACKNOWLEDGEMENT

To my Robert and Paula for your help when it comes to Harley Davidson's.

To Debbie for being my first beta reader.

This is a huge shout out to Gwen Hernandez who knows everything about Scrivener (gwenhernandez.com) and grateful for her help. Thank you.

For all my new readers - Thank you for giving this novel a chance.

If you're interested in finding out when my next novels will be out please subscribe to my newsletter at http://eepurl.com/gk8jRz and I will put you on my mailing list.

ABOUT THE AUTHOR

Living in the Santa Cruz Mountains, A.B. Cone, enjoys the peacefulness of the redwoods with her husband and son.

She enjoys her small group of friends and especially loves hanging with people that have a great sense of humor.

Loves her San Jose Sharks team when she is not yelling at the TV during a game. And even enjoys a slower paced game of baseball with her Oakland A's.

She will always try to steer her writing towards humor. Since reality from the evening news is depressing enough for anyone. Her escape is watching movies, reading her favorite romantic and paranormal novels, along with writing them. But when she's not doing any of those things she just enjoying her family.